A DEVIL'S IRON MC STORY

HEATHERED COUNTRY

PART ONE

GM SCHERBERT

DEDICATION

I WOULD LIKE TO GIVE THANKS WHERE THANKS ARE DUE. TO MY WONDERFUL AND SUPPORTIVE FAMILY AND FRIENDS WHO ARE ALWAYS THERE WITH ME TO WORK THROUGH ANY ISSUES OR PROBLEMS I WAS HAVING WITH THE BOOK, SOME MORE THAN OTHERS;) EVEN WHEN IT WAS SOMETHING THAT NORMAL PEOPLE DO NOT TALK ABOUT OVER A GLASS OF WINE OR TWO.

I LOVE YOU LONG.

I WOULD ALSO LIKE TO GIVE A SPECIAL SHOUT OUT TO ALL THE HELP I HAVE HAD WITH PROMOTING AND ALSO GETTING THE WORD OUT THERE ABOUT MY BOYS AND GIRLS. THE INDIE WORLD HAS BEEN SUPER SUPPORTIVE AND HELPFUL EVERY STEP OF THE WAY. IT ROCKS THAT Y'ALL HAVE BEEN HERE FOR ME FROM SIMPLE SWAG QUESTIONS TO FORMATTING QUESTIONS TO HELP WITH GRAPHICS AS WELL AS PROMOTING, AND EVERYTHING IN-BETWEEN...

YOU GUYS ROCK!!!

¤♥¤O°° THANKS FOR EVERYTHING °°O¤♥¤

HEATHER

When I got pregnant with Sophie, I never thought my life would get better. Each day looking over my shoulder for the man who swore when I left that he would take her from me. When I got to New Orleans and made friends with Ember, I thought my life was starting to look up.

Five years we were doing good in New Orleans, surviving as each day passed. We may be completely off of the radar from our pasts, but were doing what we want, when we want, raising the kids, and living life for ourselves. I've barely thought about him and what he had done to me, knowing I would never again give or trust myself with a man.

Then Ember's dad got sick and she went home with little Vincent. Sara and I were quick to follow with Sophie. The next thing I know I met Country and I was scared for the first time in years. I knew my heart and soul were in trouble and wasn't sure if I could take another man's rejection.

He was so nice, so easy going, I was scared that the things that I want and need are not things he would be able to give me.

Was I wrong?

Could he give me what I needed?

COUNTRY

When I moved to Chicago from Texas, I thought my life was headed exactly where it was meant to. Just because we left my dad and his wicked ways behind, and Ma and I had to come up here to stay with Grams, I knew I would find what I needed. Only thing was, I didn't know what I needed would have a daughter and be one hell of a spitfire.

The Devil's Iron brothers were quick to take me on as a prospect and quicker to put me through the paces. When I got patched in after all that shit with Pearl went down, I thought life couldn't get much better. I spend most of my nights at The Dungeon and my days running errands or doing odd jobs for the Devil's Iron.

I fall into a steady pattern. When I met my little spitfire everything changed in a flash. My mind couldn't understand what I felt for her at first, but my cock was not confused one bit. I want nothing more than to own her every want and desire.

There is next to nothing that I will not do to have her. Even if what she wants is something that I thought I would never be able to dish out, especially to a woman. For her, I will find a way.

CHAPTER
ONE

HEATHER

SEVEN YEARS AGO~

When Zack and I started dating, I thought he was such a great guy. He was the starting quarterback on our college football team and in his second year of medical school. All the girls were after him, but he only had eyes for me. He kept after me for almost six months before I finally said I would go out on a date with him. From that point on things moved exceptionally fast.

After the first year that we were together, I started to notice a change in myself. I needed more out of the relationship, more from him when we were together intimately. We had always been open and honest with each other but when I started needing more out of the sex, I found it difficult to tell him what I needed because I wasn't even sure what it was.

As I looked into what these feelings, no these desires were, I found that what I wanted, scratch that what I desired, during sex was called submission. Not necessarily submission but I craved pain when having sex. Even when I would masturbate I needed something more. Scratching myself or holding my breath would sometimes work to help me find my release but it still left me unsatisfied.

When I first brought this up to Zack he thought it might be fun to slap my ass a little during sex. Except it wasn't, he didn't do it enough: hard enough, long enough, just not enough. I tried talking with him a few more times over the months and I was never sated by what he would try. I knew that I should have left, but when I found out that I was pregnant, leaving didn't seem like an option for me any longer.

When I was pregnant with Sophie, my mood swings and hormones were all over the place. After being with him three years, the last year when I was pregnant, Zack cheated more than a few times and still he wouldn't give me what it was that I truly wanted. Some pain while we were having sex. He would call me names and fucking walk out the door when I would try to ask for more. One time we fought so bad, I thought that he would slap me in anger and I was so fucking hot and bothered, I couldn't believe that I wanted him to do that, but he didn't, and he made it more than clear that I was a fucking freak for feeling that way.

The night Sophie was born started the same as any night during those last few months. Zack calling me names and making me feel like nothing more than a freak. Like it wasn't hard enough admitting to myself what I would like to have done to my body, he had to make me feel like such a piece of shit whenever I would try to bring it up to him, which was no different that night. Heading to my room, alone, as usual I didn't realize my labor had started. I thought it was just indigestion, so I went about my nightly routine.

After a while, the pains that I was having only got worse and I decided that I needed to go to the hospital. Slowly making my way to the other side of the apartment, I knocked on the door to our spare bedroom before opening it. The sight in front of me causes me to turn quickly on my heels and head the other direction. I can't fucking believe that shit. I was in labor having that fucking piece of shit's baby and he has the nerve to be in our house, with whomever the fuck he had his dick in.

Those nights in the hospital alone with Sophie gave me plenty of time to think about my life. I am sure that after giving birth to a kid was probably not the time you should be having life changing thoughts, or is it?

Zack only came up to the hospital one time during the three days I was in there and he didn't stay more than fifteen minutes. He told me that he had shit to do and he would see me when I got back to the apartment. He didn't even hold Sophie, let alone barely look at her. Which would have broken my fucking heart, if it hadn't already been shattered by him these last few months. I can't believe that the only man I had ever been with, the man that I gave my heart, my virginity, my all to was such a complete and utter piece of shit.

A few weeks after Sophie was born I'd had enough of Zack and the changes that had slowly been happening in him. Even though Zack didn't want me or the baby, he wouldn't let me leave. He never had a problem telling me how he would take her away if I ever left him, and it scared me enough that when I ran it was in the middle of the night. I knew never to look back.

I found myself in New Orleans, thankful I had a couple of friends who had come here after graduation. They helped me out with Sophie when I found a job. The small one-bedroom apartment that I had was in a bad neighborhood, but I knew how to take care of myself. When I met Ember almost a year later, I knew she was in a bad way and running from something. I was happy to help her out and although we didn't share our troubles with each other we formed a tight bond over our troubled pasts.

CHAPTER
TWO

COUNTRY

GROWING UP~

As far back as I can remember I have lived surrounded by the brotherhood of an MC. My dad was part of the Demon Riders in Texas while I was growing up. As soon as I was old enough to be away from my ma and on my own I was with my dad at the clubhouse. From what I saw and can remember of them, their shit was as dirty as it got. Women, drugs, dog fights, guns, and any other thing that they could make money on was flowing freely.

I use to idolize my dad and would enjoy hanging out with him and the Demon Riders. Once I got to be about ten though, I started to understand what the fuck was going on and shit quickly changed. The shit he and his brothers were doing actually started clicking inside my head and I saw how fucked up it really was.

I'm not talking about the drinking and the whores at the clubhouse, that shit is common place. No, what I'm talking about is the drugs, the guns, the fucking dog fights, and the flesh dealers that they had running rampant. The way most of those brothers treated a woman always left a sour taste in my mouth. I thought my dad was better, that he would never treat a woman, let alone my mother that way. I was fucking wrong.

A week or two after my tenth birthday I came home from school and found Ma with a black eye. It was the first time that I ever noticed, but I knew that it was not the first time it happened. Even then, thinking back I couldn't help but know how wrong it was to put your hands on a woman. Why the fuck would a man ever do that? A real man wouldn't ever do that shit. Not to his woman, his old lady, his wife.

After coming home to that on and off for about two months, I finally decided enough was enough. But, my ten-year-old self was no challenge for the man that is my father. The first time I tried to get between him and my mother, I was put in the hospital for two weeks. That shit never stopped me though. I was in and out of hospitals for the next four years of my life, until puberty kicked in at fourteen and I started to be a little bit too much for him to handle. He went back to hitting on Ma, only when I was at school though, which did a fucking number on my attendance because I never knew when he would get in one of his moods.

I still hung around the clubhouse but usually only when he was on a run, passed out, or had some club whore in his room. The brothers were waiting for me to finish high school so that I could start prospecting, and follow along in my old man's footsteps. Little did they know that was the fucking last thing that I wanted to do. I mean I love the MC life, or at least the thought of it, the way the Demon Riders lived it for the most part was fucking wrong though. You don't fight dogs for fucking sport, you don't fucking involve yourself and your club in the flesh trade, and you sure as fuck don't put your hands on or mark your woman, for any fucking reason.

I don't know why Ma didn't leave his ass sooner, because she had to have known about the shit that was going on with him when he was away. I am not sure why it was never talked about, everyone knew what the fuck was going on. My mom wanted to protect me from the shit that happened between her and Dad, but that just never happened. Not until the night she came close to death and we got the fuck outta there.

I was gonna turn seventeen in a month, well over six-foot-tall and pushing two-fifty of pure muscle. Dad didn't get near mom unless he knew damn good and well that I wouldn't be home anytime soon. I hadn't seen any signs on her for going on a year, ever since I walked in on him hitting her and I broke his arm. I told him if I caught him with his hands on Ma again I would fucking end him, and he kept away, at least I thought he did.

That night as we left, Ma let me know that it had continued the whole time, just not where I could see. He had moved on to hitting her in places that he knew damn well I wouldn't see, breaking ribs and puncturing at least one of her lungs on occasion. I lose no sleep thinking of what I did to that man, knowing that he will never hurt Ma again is all I need to know.

As far back as I can remember, I have lived surrounded by the brotherhood of an MC. My dad was part of the Demon

Riders in Texas while I was growing up. As soon as I was old enough to be away from my ma and on my own, I was with my dad at the Clubhouse. From what I saw and can remember of them, their shit was as dirty as it got. Women, drugs, dog fights, guns, and any other thing that they could make money on, was flowing freely.

I idolized my dad back then, and until I really started to understand what the fuck was going on, I really liked hanging out with him and all the Demon Riders. Once I got to be about ten though, shit changed and changed quick. The shit his brothers and him were doing actually started clicking inside my head, and I saw how fucked up it really was. I'm not talking about the drinking and the whores at the Clubhouse, that shit is common place.

I'm talking about the drugs, the guns, the fucking dog fights, and the flesh dealers that they had running rampant. The way most of those brothers treated a woman always left a sour taste in my mouth. I thought my dad was better, that he would never treat a woman, let alone my mother that way. I was fucking wrong.

A week or two after my tenth birthday I came home from school and found Ma with a black eye. It was the first time that I ever noticed, but I knew that it was not the first time it happened. Even then, thinking back I couldn't help but know how wrong it was to put your hands on a woman. Why the fuck would a man ever do that? A real man wouldn't ever do that shit. Not to his woman, his old lady, his wife.

After coming home to that on and off for about two months, I finally decided enough was enough. But, my ten-year-old self was no challenge for the man that is my father. The first time I tried to get between him and my mother, I was put in the hospital for two weeks. That shit never stopped me though. I was in and out of hospitals for the next four years of my life, until puberty kicked in at fourteen and I started to be a little bit too much for him to handle. He went back to hitting on Ma, only when I was at school though, which did a fucking number on my attendance because I never knew when he would get in one of his moods.

I still hung around the Clubhouse but usually only when he was on a run, passed out, or had some club whore in his room. The brothers were waiting for me to finish high school so that I could start prospecting, and follow along in my old man's footsteps. Little did they know that was the fucking last thing that I wanted to do. I mean I love the MC life, or at least the thought of it, the way the Demon Riders lived it for the most part was fucking wrong though. You don't fight dogs for fucking sport, you don't fucking involve yourself and your club in the flesh trade, and you sure as fuck don't put your hands on or mark your woman, for any fucking reason.

I don't know why Ma didn't leave his ass sooner, because she had to have known about the shit that was going on with him when he was away. I am not sure why it was never talked about, everyone knew what the fuck was going on. My mom wanted to protect me from the shit that happened between her and Dad, but that just never happened. Not until the night she came close to death and we got the fuck outta there.

I was gonna turn seventeen in a month, well over six-foot-tall and pushing two-fifty of pure muscle. Dad didn't get near mom unless he knew damn good and well that I wouldn't be home anytime soon. I hadn't seen any signs on her for going on a year, ever since I walked in on him hitting her and I broke his arm. I told him if I caught him with his hands on Ma again I would fucking end him, and he kept away, at least I thought he did.

That night as we left, Ma let me know that it had continued the whole time, just not where I could see. He had moved on to hitting her in places that he knew damn well I wouldn't see, breaking ribs and puncturing at least one of her lungs on occasion. I lose no sleep thinking of what I did to that man, knowing that he will never hurt Ma again is all I need to know.

CHAPTER
THREE

HEATHER

FIVE YEARS AGO~

Finding myself working at a bar in New Orleans I know that living off the grid is the best way to keep Zack away. Those last few weeks with him were really fucking hard. I knew it was the time to leave when he was fucking other women in our home, while our fucking daughter was home. There is only so much that one person can take.

When I met Ember I knew that she was running from something. She didn't really talk about herself those first few weeks, hell the first months really, but I knew she was hiding some dark secrets. Within a week of meeting, she had moved into my place, seeing that I couldn't let her pregnant ass live in her car any longer. On the couch of the crappy one bedroom I live in is not the way she should be going through her pregnancy, but it's all we can do, for now.

As the months pass, and Ember's friend Sara decides to move down with us, we end up moving into a bigger apartment. An apartment that Ember, Sophie, Sara, Vincent, and I all fit into much better. The time starts passing with little more than the blink of an eye. When the three of us are finally settled in and comfortable with our new lives, I finally feel comfortable enough to start exploring more of myself and the woman that I need to be. Having Ember and Sara around to help with Sophie I long for a relationship, no not a relationship I will never do that shit again, I long for pain.

I start to realize and remember what I need from a man, what Zack thought was so unnatural, so disgusting, so wrong. I tried to find the relief that I needed on my own, and that only led to lots of sessions with Tonya at the local shop where Sara has been working part time. She has pierced me in ways that I didn't even think were possible, and multiple at a time. The worst of those days was the day she pierced my lips and clit within minutes of each other. After that day the pain I needed was sated, for a few weeks at least. After that last day of piercing my body in the last of my free "typical" spots, Tonya and I moved on to tattoos. She has also given me well over twenty tattoos in the five years I have been in New Orleans, ten of which probably in the first year. Finding myself at the door of the shop every few weeks with an idea and the need for the pain.

Tonya is the one that introduced me to Club Coquin, the BDSM club she belongs too. As I think back on those first times, I knew it was only a way to deal with the turmoil I felt inside. Tonya got me the right introductions, paperwork, and such but told me that if it was something that I wanted I would need to do it on my own. Seeing hurt in her eyes I think that something must have happened to have her acting this way. She lets me know that she is always here to talk if needed, but she just can't go to the club anymore.

I was nervous as fuck the first time I went into Club Coquin by myself, but those nerves were set at ease by a woman, a Domme named Mistress Diamond. She helped not only me, but Ember and Sara as well, not only that first night but for the years that we were still in New Orleans. Although she tried those first few times, Mistress was never able to get me kneeling comfortably at her feet. I found over the years that submission is not something that has ever done anything for me sexually. Kneeling for someone, following their every command and rules is just not me, at least I have never found someone that I feel comfortable giving myself to like that. It didn't work for Mistress Diamond or any of the men that tried over the years at Club Coquin.

I found quickly that pain, on the other hand, can force me to my knees in just about any situation. When I had brought it up with Zack, he would belittle me and make me feel so small, I thought the way I was feeling t was wrong. The first time I negotiated a scene at Club Coquin it had me thinking that Zack might have been right. The Dom that I negotiated the scene with was handsome and strong, and made me feel nothing for him sexually. It was a surreal experience to say the least.

When the Dom approached me I was sitting by myself at the bar. He looked down to my bracelets and saw that I was new and wanted to explore my pain thresholds. The gleam in his eyes at the realization had me second guessing myself. Looking up he meets my eyes before extending his hand to me.

"Hello, I'm Master Finn." Extending my hand, tingles shoot up my arm when our skin touches and I wonder instantly what the fuck that is. "Whatever is your story, Pumpkin?"

"My name is Heather, actually."

"Hmm. I like Pumpkin, you don't mind if I call you that for our time together, do you?"

Meeting his eyes, I look directly into them as I answer, "Well, I guess that is fine, Finn."

Looking down to my wrist the smile widens on his face before his eyes reach mine again and he goes on. "You don't seem to have a submissive bone in your body, do you Pumpkin?"

"No, that I do not Finn."

Releasing my hand Finn slides into the seat next to me. "Whatever are you doing here then, Pumpkin? I can see by your bracelets that you are new to the scene and that you are exploring pain which is an odd combination if I do say so myself." Pointing around to the few scenes that are going on throughout the room, he looks back to me before continuing. "Most people that are exploring pain would have already been in this scene for a bit to have some bases of what they were getting themselves in to. You however, just cut right to the chase, huh?"

"Yes, well. I have been here a few times before and figured out rather quickly that kneeling isn't something that gets me going. I have experimented with pain on my own though and it is something that I can always count on to get my pussy all hot and bothered."

Moving his hand quickly to the pulse point in my neck, he answers only after leaning into me. "You, Pumpkin, are truly a rarity. I think I would like to take you to a room and see what you can truly handle."

"I think I might like that as well, Finn."

"Pumpkin, let's talk about your limitations for tonight. You should always be able to talk with anyone that you scene with, if you can't then they are not a good fit for you. If you are not able to be open and honest, leave the scene immediately, understand me Pumpkin?"

"Yes Finn, I understand what you're saying. I know that talking with my partner is always something that should be done before each scene. My only limitation this evening is that I do not want to be penetrated. I will suck your cock if you so desire, but I do not wish to have sex. The rush of endorphins from the pain is all I need to feel free." Looking towards this man, I add, "My safe words are red, yellow, and green and I will have no problem using them if need be."

Running his hand down my arm, he grabs my hand as he says, "Well, Pumpkin let's go and see what we can figure out about those pain limits that you want to know about. Shall we?"

Pulling me behind him down the hallway, I make note of the people we pass on our way to the room. Cries of pleasure and pain move quickly past my ears as we walk. Coming to the last door at the end of the hallway, Finn turns to me, "It's not too late for you Pumpkin. If you would like to turn back around now, I would be more than willing to see you home safely."

"Thanks but no thanks Finn. I am good right where I am, in fact I will be great in just a second." Pushing the door open I walk into the room and pause briefly seeing the décor of the room. Crops, floggers, belts, paddles, canes, and lots of other deviousness is hanging on every open space of this room. When my feet catch up to my mind, I move over to the wall slowly running my fingers over a beautifully colored flogger.

"That is one of my favorites, Pumpkin. I am not sure that you will be able to handle the cut from that one on our first go, but we will see. Strip outta those clothes for me so I can see what I'm working with."

Slowly turning I remove the tight shirt that I am wearing, before slipping from my bra and exposing my breasts to him. The rings that I have in my nipples are suddenly so heavy that I can feel the pull on the tightening buds. Slowly running my hands over my body, I slip my fingers under the waist of my skirt and slide it down my legs before raising my eyes up to his.

Slowly straightening back up, I hear his voice as my hands reach the edge of my barley there panties. "No, Pumpkin, leave that slip of underwear on. I want to see you soaking them like you say you will when the pain starts. It will also help to remind me that we are taking this no further than this." Adjusting himself through his leathers he adds almost to himself, "No matter what my cock might have in mind."

Finn positions me face forward onto the cross then lays an assortment of tools onto the bed before coming back to me. Using a rough rope, Finn secures my hands before skimming his hands down my legs, pulling first one than the other ankle to secure them to the cross as well. Watching him walk back to the bed, my breath catches as he picks up first a flogger throwing it casually over his left shoulder. As it is tossed over his shoulder I notice that something on the ends of it catches the overhead lights and only then do I realize that it has beads or something at the end of it. Reaching for a whip Finn threads it through his right arm, having it come to rest over his shoulder as he looks from me back to the toys. Lastly he reaches for and grabs up a thick wooden paddle that had a large heart carved out of the middle.

"Warming you up with this is going to give me nothing but the utmost pleasure," he says spinning the paddle around in his hand while walking from the bed towards me. "Stick that pretty ass of yours out Pumpkin and let's see how much pain you can really handle."

Throwing my ass out as much as possible while being bound to the cross is more difficult than you would think. As I settle in to a comfortable position, and I use that term loosely, I take a few deep breaths waiting for the first strike to land. It is long minutes before anything happens and during that time I lose myself to the thoughts in my head.

Thoughts of Zack and the way he used to talk to me, the way he used to call me names, and belittle me for telling him what it was that I wanted, no needed.

The first tap with the paddle and I almost laugh out loud at the strength this man must have held back to land it.

"Finn, you are going to need to do better than that."

That must egg him on because the next tap with the paddle definitely leaves an impression on me. The force that it landed with causes me to have to catch myself from spilling the contents of my stomach. As he lands a few more with the paddle I know that the heart will leave an impression on my ass for long days to come, and I cannot help myself from moaning out. "Yes please, more like that Finn."

I hear the paddle hit the floor before I shift from one foot to the other, waiting for the next thing to be used on me. After the first strike I know that he has moved on to the flogger. The beads that I caught glistening as he threw it over his shoulder are making an impact on me and as he moves over not only my ass but my back and thighs as well, I am brought closer to the edge. I am starting to drift off at the thuds from the flogger when I am startled back from wherever I was headed by the crack of what I can only guess is the whip that Finn had put over his shoulder.

"You have taken those so nicely, Pumpkin. Now, we will see if you are truly the pain slut that you claim to be or if you are just a glutton for punishment."

After the first strike lands I have thoughts that this might not truly be for me. With the next few strikes the cry I hear I don't even recognize as my own. The tenth lash lands and the pain I feel causes a hitch in my throat that has me struggling to keep the contents of my stomach there. By the twentieth strike I find myself floating and can only hear what sounds like far-off voices before the binding at my wrist and ankles are removed and I am gently carried to the bed. Slowly coming back around I feel Finn rubbing my wrists and ankles as I come back around and hear him saying "So gorgeous, you are flying for me Pumpkin."

As I come back down to Earth, Finn talks me through my first subspace. He goes into great detail about my endorphins and how I should handle the feelings that I am having. He also tells me that I was more than correct about my need for pain. That I am the first one to be able to take him at his full force, that I will make some man a fucking fine pain slut when I decide to take on the roll for good. As he hands me my clothing and as I am getting dressed he lets me know that any time I feel the need for pain, he will be more than willing to help.

Over the next four years I return to Club Coquin at least monthly for a "cleansing" as I have come to call them. The way I felt each time I had a scene at Club Coquin I knew that Zack could not have been further from the truth. I fucking loved the way being spanked, paddled, whipped, flogged, or caned made me feel. I almost always felt nothing but joy when a session was over. There being only two times that the scene was something that it should not have been, leaving me with bruises from fists out of anger and hate. Both of those times the bouncers were quick to step in and remove the Doms that felt the need to step over the boundaries of the club. Both times, I knew in my heart that these men weren't sadists they were sick fucks that wanted to beat a woman senseless.

After a few sessions with Finn at the beginning, I went off and found others that cared to scene with me as well. Sometimes I return to a partner for more than one session, but I have never had sex with any of them. That seems too personal to me, I know it's fucked up when I am naked and spread open to these men and women, that penetration is where I draw the line. Many have made me come repeatedly with their hands or mouths, but never has a cock or even a strap on or dildo been inside of me.

Each Dom or Domme thinks that they will be the one to bring this pain slut to her knees and yet, I have never safe-worded and never allowed any of them closer to my heart.

CHAPTER FOUR

COUNTRY

SEVEN YEARS AGO~

When Ma and I moved up north by Grams, I didn't know that my life would fall into place like it did. Finishing off my senior year when we got to Chicago, I didn't make many friends those last few months of school. That summer I spent much of my time hanging around the mechanic that was a few doors down from Grams house. He let me work the front, but would teach me about the cars and bikes that would come in after hours. When he encouraged me to go to the Tech College and get my degree I didn't hesitate. Staying on with Grams to help her out as I went to school, I graduated two short years later. When the house next door to Grams opened up I didn't hesitate to buy it, so I could keep an eye on her.

Continuing to work at that neighborhood garage, I made fast friends with a few bikers that would bring their bikes into the shop occasionally. After talking to them for a while, they invited me to come hang out at their clubhouse for a party and to meet some of their brothers. Going on twenty-one, I decide that a stroll down memory lane being at a clubhouse again, would be nostalgic.

When I first walked into the clubhouse I felt a peace come over me, that I had not felt since we left Texas, before the shit went down with my dad at the end. I felt at home and it only grew the more time I spent hanging around the Devil's Iron. For the next three years, I spent more and more time at the clubhouse, until I finally made the decision that this brotherhood was nothing like the one I had grown up in. The years I had been around Blaze, Tank, Doc, Gun, Shadow, and the others were eye opening to me. All MC's were not run as shitty and illegally as the Demon Riders were. Thank fuck.

That time was one that I look back on as changing my life. I decided then and there that I wanted that way of life, free flowing drinks, woman at the ready, and a brotherhood that would be there for you through thick and thin. I found a sponsor and started prospecting after those years of being a friend and hang around to them.

Being a prospect to all the members is shit, it's nothing more than being a glorified bitch, but it's what I needed to do to get where I want to be. One of the first big jobs that I had to do for the MC was looking out for and over the Prez's old lady, Pearl. She had gotten herself mixed up in a fucking shit of a situation and was in need of some watching. It was nothing more than glorified babysitting, that was until it all turned to shit.

It started when Tick, one of the other prospects shoved his way into Pearl's home and Prez took offence to it. Not that I wouldn't have done the same fucking thing for someone putting their hands on what was mine. Prez brought him outside and showed him what the fuck happens when you touch something that doesn't belong to you.

A few nights later, Bull and I were sent to watch over Pearl as the brothers went to get her kids, Iris and Rose back from Tick and Layla. I was pissed that I didn't get to go along, but we are only fucking prospects and so babysitting, again, it is.

As Bull and I get inside the house Pearl lets us know that we should make ourselves at home. She says that she is going to go outside and cool off a little and after Bull tries to go with her, I have to chime in.

Walking towards the kitchen to grab something to eat, I tell Pearl. "Grab your coat on the way out, I don't want to have Prez climbing up my ass if you catch a cold or some other shit."

I guess that Pearl must not have liked that because she was quick to return, "Fuck, you guys are treating me like I am a fucking baby or some shit. I am a grown ass fucking woman with two, no, three kids, actually and old enough to probably be at least one of your mothers, so you can cut the over protective shit out and just let me be."

Looking towards Pearl I answer her sharply. "No, Pearl we won't do that. Prez wants you safe and we are here to see to that, so don't ask us to break our word to him. Being disloyal to this club is just something that we wouldn't do. We are prospecting with the Devil's Iron because we want to be part of the brotherhood. We would not do anything to go against what any of the brothers want, that is the reason for the brotherhood."

Bull continues on before I can catch my breath or thoughts. "I agree with Country. That is one reason that what Tick did is so fucked up. He put his hands on you, Pearl, that is something that he should not ever have done, then plotting with Layla and following through with this fucking scheme to take the girls. If Prez didn't have those bugs and trackers in both yours and Ticks vehicles we would have had no fucking idea where the girls are, so thank fuck he was being over protective with you."

I can tell that we have spent too much time together recently when I continue on for him without as much as a moments pause. "Don't even get me started on what that fucker Tank did to you those months back." Cracking my knuckles thinking back to those events of that night, I take a deep breath before continuing. "That shit was fucked up and when I see him, I have a few things that I need to fucking say to him before letting Prez get a hold of him."

Pearl grabs up her coat and head towards the back door. Both Bull and I watch as she steps out of the back door. Moving towards the garage she pulls out a lawn chair and sits in the moon light. Bull heads off to use the can and after a few more minutes a car passes through the alley, I move back into the kitchen and grab some food. Walking back towards the back window, I notice movement near the gate and see Pearl is no longer in her lawn chair. Throwing the food down, I holler for Bull, flip on the back light, and head out the back door towards Pearl. The scene that is playing out before Bull and I, is one that has me questioning if this woman even needs our protection.

Pearl is on top of Layla, striking her repeatedly with her fists. I speak as I make my way towards her, but I'm sure that she is not hearing or understanding a word that I am speaking. When I finally reach them, I pull Pearl off of Layla as gently as possible before Bull is able to lift Layla's limp body off of the cement. As Bull heads toward the garage with Layla I usher Pearl into the house towards the bathroom so that she can clean herself up. Shutting the door behind her I head back outside to Bull and the situation that we have just gotten thrust headfirst into.

Opening the garage door, I find that Bull has tied Layla to a chair and placed a drop cloth under her. She has multiple bruises and cuts all over her face and the blood is pooling under her. Looking towards Bull, we speak only briefly before deciding that Prez needs to be called immediately. As I turn to head to the door to grab my phone, I am met instead by Pearl. She walks into the garage past us and grabs a bat. She looks towards us pointing the bat at us as she tries to tell us that we need to leave and go check on the house and see if Blaze has tried to reach out to them.

"Pearl, I don't think that Prez would want you to do that, especially in your current condition." I get out before Bull cuts me off.

"I am just going to talk with her, County. Go in the house and check to see if he has contacted you or if Doc is on his way back with the girls." She says to us, slowly walking around to the front of Layla, who looks up at her.

"Ok, but hand me the bat before I go. I don't want you to do something that Blaze would be pissed about." Is all I can think to say, knowing that we need to update Prez about the current situation. Extending my hand, I wait patiently for Pearl to hand me the bat.

As she slowly places the bat in my hand she growls out, "This bitch is the reason that I was raped and beaten. She is also the reason that my children were taken tonight, and I still haven't heard if they have been found or if they are hurt." Seeing the hurt in her eyes, I think only briefly that this might not be the right course of action. As we turn to leave we shut the garage door behind us before quickly heading to the house to grab the phone and make our way back to the garage.

Walking quickly to the house, I grab my cell off the counter and place a call to Blaze. Prez hollers an answer into the phone as he picks up and I can hear the fucking anger in his voice. "What is it Country, I am somewhat busy right now, this better be good."

 Rubbing a hand over my chin, I roll my eyes and answer. "Prez we have a visitor here at the house. You might want to hurry before Pearl gets rid of her by herself."

He disconnections the phone and I go to let Bull know what is going on before heading back out the door towards the garage. A few steps before I hit the back door of the house on my way back outside, when my phone starts ringing. Pulling the phone from my pocket, I see that Prez is calling and don't even have a chance to speak before he barks out, "Country go get Pearl and put her on the phone."

Opening the back door, I jog up to the garage before pulling the door open. Growling at the scene before me I raise my voice slightly, "Pearl, what the fuck have you been doing in here? You said you were just going to talk to her. Fucking hell, here take the phone; Prez wants to talk to you."

Trying not to eavesdrop I turn to look at Layla and my eyes widen at the sight. Hearing Bull coming into the garage, I hear the small groan that comes out of him as he takes in the scene before us. Layla is close to death and I know that Pearl can never know what happened in here. Even if she remembers beating her and hitting her with that rebar, she will never know that she was the one that dealt the death blow.

Hearing the rebar drop to the cement floor, my eyes move up to Pearl and I see the rage slowly leave her face before she shuffles out of the garage, handing me the phone on her way out.

"Prez, she dropped what she was doing and is heading into the house. Do you want me to have Bull go inside to get eyes on her?" is all I can think to say as Bull starts trying to check over Layla's injuries.

Bull stands hearing what I have just told Prez, as I switch the phone over to speaker we hear his answer. "No, you two sit on the visitor, we will be there in just a few minutes. I will come to check in with you as soon as we get there while Doc gets the girls into the house. See you in a few."

As I end the call, Bull and I look at each other. He is the first to speak but his thoughts mirror my own.

"Bitch got what she fucking deserved."

"That she did brother, that she did. I'm hoping her brother and Tick went the same way."

"Nah, I bet that they took them over to the house on the drive to put them down. We will know as soon as Prez gets here."

Looking around the garage I hear the van pull up outside and start wondering how much shit we are about to be in for. Prez walks into the garage and eyes up the scene. Looking from me towards Bull he asks quickly, "What the fuck has been going on in here, Bull?"

Bull answers shrugging his shoulders, "Pearl, Prez. When Layla crept down the alley she pulled a gun on Pearl and forced her way into the yard with her. By the time we got to them, Pearl had her on the ground and was straddling her beating her with her fists. We pulled her off of Layla and I had her go into the house to shower, but by the time we had Layla situated in the garage Pearl came back out. She grabbed a bat and told us to go in the house and get a hold of you, we took the bat from her, but she found the rebar and used it" pointing to the heap on the chair, "to do that."

Seeing the anger rise up from Prez I know we are in for it. "You listened to her? What the fuck, did you think it was a smart move to let a pregnant woman, my fucking pregnant woman be alone with her? You know that is not something that I would have allowed. Why the fuck was she in the backyard by herself anyways? You two were supposed to be watching her. FUCK! Clean this shit up and load her into the van and get her to the house on the Drive. The others have taken the three we found there as well. I will be there as soon as I get the situation with Pearl worked out and we can show them the proper welcome."

As we clean up the mess that Pearl made, and get Layla into the van I see that she is gone. Reaching for her eyes I close them quickly giving her the respect that she didn't deserve in life. I know that Pearl should never know what she did tonight, she has been too affected by the events of the last few months and that shit will not be good for the baby.

We make our way over to the house on the Drive and get the men situated in the basement, waiting for Prez to come so we can take care of these fuckers. I look around to the men that are here waiting for the judgement that Prez sees fit to hand down. As I look towards Trip, my feet move in his direction as I speak lowly, "What's gonna happen here, Trip? Is Prez gonna put these fucking fools down like he should have done the night that they attacked Pearl?"

"Country, that is only for him to decide. It was his family that they went after, and his woman that they fucking violated. If it were me though, and that was my woman that they had done that fucking shit to, those fuckers would have their skin peeled from their bodies."

"Yeah, I know what you're saying. My dad used to beat on my ma and I go crazy thinking about violence towards a woman." Looking around to the others brothers that are in the basement, I notice that no one is paying attention to us, so I go on. "It's why I have a hard time at The Dungeon some times. Some of those scenes are almost too much for me. When the subs are fighting tooth and nail and the Doms are really hurting them." Shaking my head, I continue on, "I don't think I would ever be able to do that to my ol' lady."

"Country, it's different than that and you should probably talk to one of the guys at The Dungeon about the differences, Shadow would probably lend a hand. Especially if you are not seeing what happens at The Dungeon as anything more than domestic violence. It is far from that."

Nodding my head at that, I walk away and think about what Trip has said. I know that those women are ok with everything that happens at The Dungeon, but it still doesn't sit well with me. Maybe he is right that I should talk with Shadow. Lost in my thoughts, I don't notice that it takes over an hour for Prez to walk through the garage of the house on the Drive. Walking into the basement, Bull and Trip are standing next to me as I let Prez know that the room is all set and that Tick is the only one talking.

"Tick won't shut the fuck up about how he was not involved, he is a Devil and he would never do anything against us, that he was taken and didn't fucking do anything to that cunts stupid kids." As a growl leaves him I add, "His words not mine Prez."

Seeing the rage consuming Prez, I know I would never like to be on the receiving end of that look. He stalks toward Tick who is strapped down onto a chair in the middle of the basement. He takes the hammer to first one and then the other of Tick's knees and then speaks. "You never should have fucked with my ol' lady or her kids. You will never have the chance to do it again or prove yourself as anything more than the sorry fucking coward that you are." Picking up the axe, the sound of the swing and the

35

way the bone cracks on impact causes my stomach to lurch. Prez adds, "See you in Hell, mother fucker."

As Prez looks around the room towards each brother, he nods and the smiles come to our faces. Knowing that he has given us each a chance to pay back these fuckers for what they did not only to Pearl but the girls as well. Each Devil in the basement gets a turn at bloodying these stupid fucks to a pulp. As the last brother takes his turn at these two stupid fucks, we all look to Prez waiting to see what his next move will be. I know both these fuckers are about to die, but it is up to Prez as to how that happens.

Prez answers the unasked question quickly after reaching out and taking a gun from Trip. "Anyone who wants to stay and help, please do so, anyone else head upstairs and have a few drinks, smoke some weed, and get a good night's sleep so this can get cleaned up tomorrow and these bodies can be put to ground."

Not one of the brothers move, we all turn shaking our heads at Prez, before Trip speaks. "No, Prez. We want to do this for Pearl, Iris, and Rose. She is your ol' lady and they are as much our family as they are your's, so we will all stay and put these fucks down."

Each of us draw out our weapons, and aim towards the two men. Prez gives a quick nod as we let loose on these fuckers that have hurt Pearl, and in turn Prez so much. Placing the guns into a bag that has been set up on the corner of the tarp we take off our boots and head upstairs to clean up.

CHAPTER
FIVE

HEATHER

The last five years in New Orleans has really helped me become a stronger, more independent, mother and woman. The time I spend with Sara and Ember has really helped to make me who I am, those bitches really give me a lot of support and love. They watch over Sophie when I need a little time to myself, and have even supported me in my choices about my love life, or lack thereof. The time that I have spent both with Tonya at the shop and at Club Coquin has also helped. The relief and freedom that I find through the pain is something that I cannot and have not been able to find anywhere else or through anything else.

 When Ember got the call about her father getting ill, she and Vincent left quickly to return to Chicago. Both Sara and I keep in close contact with her, knowing that being back in Chicago, where Doc was, would be hard for her. As Sara and I continued our lives in New Orleans, we joked about moving up North and getting our "little family" back together. Fuck that shit, I hate the snow and cold. That is until the day I got a message from Zack.

The text message was simple and it scared the ever loving shit outta me.

UNKNOWN: *I am coming. You should have never ran away, you stupid cunt.*

Knowing that my luck with Zack has run out, I talk with Sara about moving that same night. I tell her that I don't care where we go, but that we need to stay off the grid and get the fuck outta here. She thinks that I am joking and when she looks at me and only sees fear in my eyes she agrees, instantly. She knows about my past and Sophie's dad so when she guesses why I am in such a rush to get outta New Orleans I don't lie to her. I let her know about the text and it takes her one night after me bringing it up, to come up with a plan to get us out of New Orleans.

"Heather, what do you think about moving up to Chicago? I think that I would like to go home and be able to spend some time with Irene. The tenants in my house are due out at the end of the month, so we will have a place to stay. What do you think?"

"You sure about that, Sara? I know that you want to see Irene and make these last few years up to her, but, what about Gun? I thought that you were never going to go back there and fall in with him or that MC lifestyle again?"

"Yeah, yeah I know I said that, but I think I will be able to deal with the situation. It's been five years for fucks sake, I'm sure he doesn't even have the time of day to think about the past. The end of the month is two weeks away, can we wait that long? Or do we need to get a move on sooner?"

"I think Sophie and I will take a little road trip and meet you up there in a few weeks. We need to get a move on, like now, I don't want Zack catching up to us."

"Okay girl, let's get your shit packed up and I will ship it up to my house." Seeing the worry cross my face she doesn't hesitate to continue, "Don't worry I have done this shit before, it will be okay. I am not sure how he tracked you here, but we will give him the slip again. Okay?"

Trying to let the worry slip away, a forced smile crosses my face. "I know Sara, I just worry about Sophie and what would happen if something happened to me or if he got his hands on her."

"No worries about that Heather, once we get to Chicago I will get you all set up at my place," seeing the fear cross my eyes, she goes on, "until you find a place of your own of course. I will even put a call into the hospital and see if I can get you a job, if you want?"

Smiling towards her, "That would be great Sara. I will look around too; I don't want to have to rely on you for everything. That would make me feel like a burden and you know how I feel about that shit." Turning I make my way to my bedroom and slowly start packing up the belongings I will need for our trip in my suitcase, and my other belongings for the move.

Making my way to both Club Coquin as well as the tattoo shop, I let the few friends that I have made know I will be leaving. That I will reach out when I can to let them know that I am okay. Having people worry about me is something that had only recently started, so I wanted to make sure that they would not be left high and dry. Each in their own way gave me a sense of calm, serenity, and peace that I didn't think could be taken from me. Letting me be who I should be and not making me feel any less of a person for it. I came into my own skin these last years, and I am more than able to be comfortable with who I have become. But, Zack threatening to take that all away from me, just does something to the security that I have been building.

Knowing that Zack wouldn't be able to find me again, for a while at least, we leave early the next day. We head around from Florida to New York and finally head towards Chicago with the cash that I could pull out of the bank. Switched cars frequently paid only cash for everything and lived completely off the grid for the three weeks we were in the wind. My heart will never be given away like the mistake that I had made with Zack.

Not until I was in Chicago and saw him for the first time did I know that I was in trouble and that I had been completely wrong about my heart. It was far from unbreakable.

CHAPTER
SIX

COUNTRY

These last few months have gone by in a blur. After the shit went down with Pearl, the brothers voted me and Bull in quick. Things were hairy for a bit between all the brothers and Tank, but when the brothers found out that Pearl had forgiven him, they followed suit. It has been something to watch them together. Most of the brothers in this club are settling down and it's something that I can't imagine happening to me. The club girls are always around and I can't see needing more than the release that I find from them. Bull and I have taken women together on occasion and I can't imagine many women like Pearl out there who would be okay with it. I'm not even thirty yet and I don't think I could see myself being tied down to one woman, especially considering if I ever made that commitment, it would be the only one I ever make.

My runs keep me out for longer than I am home, and that's why I haven't been to check up on Grams in a while, I just got back from another run yesterday. I miss her and know that before heading to the clubhouse for the wedding tonight, I will drop by and catch up with her for a bit, looking to the clock I see that its ten in the morning and Grams will be watching her shows, so I throw on my boots and Stetson walking out the door of my place and head next door.

Not even pausing to knock, I enter her house and am greeted by her sitting on the couch doing exactly what I thought she would be, watching her show with a cup of coffee. Turning her head towards me a smiles crosses her face as she greets me, "Wayne, it has been too long, get over here and give me a kiss."

Striding towards her, I stop her before she can get herself up, bending down to wrap her up in my arms. "Grams, I have asked you not to call me that, you know how much I hate that name. It doesn't suit me."

"John Wayne was a great man, your parents loved the classics and thought it would suit you. I didn't agree at the time, but look at you. You wear those boots and hat so well."

"Ugh, Grams. How have you been? I know that mom has come to check up on you a few times while I have been gone these last couple days. You need anything?"

"No Wayne, I'm good, your Ma comes to check on me every day when you are outta town. She was actually here this morning and brought over some groceries for me. Could you go grab me a beer though? This one is," she says wiggling her empty coffee cup at me.

"Grams, its ten in the morning-"

"So? I'm not telling you that you have to have one." She says shooing me into the kitchen, I end up grabbing one for her and two for me. There is no way in hell I'm gonna let my Grams drink alone.

Walking back into the living room, I hand Grams her beer and sit down on the couch with her. "Here you go Grams. There is a wedding at the clubhouse tonight and then tomorrow when I come home, I will get to the yard and stuff. I'm gonna sit and watch with you for a little while before I gotta get going, if that's alright?"

"Wedding, who is getting married? Is it that lovely woman Pearl? Her and those men of hers are something. I never thought that someone could have so much love in their heart, but those three really can't be without each other."

I nod my head, thinking back to the few family BBQ's that Grams has come to in the last few years. She met Pearl briefly at the one she came to with Tank and then has seen her again at one with Blaze. She brought up how odd it was that a woman could have such strong feeling for two different men. When I asked her about it when we were at the last BBQ a few months back, she only said, "When you know it's right you just know. That woman has nothing but love in her eyes, for both of those men and even though it's not tradition they make each other happy and that's all that matters."

"Are you taking a date to the BBQ, Wayne?" a smile spreads across her lips as she looks towards me.

"Nah, Grams. You know that the clubhouse isn't really the place to bring dates. I will probably just hang out with the brothers, and maybe talk to one of the girls there."

"Those fucking club whores." Spitting the sip of beer outta my mouth at her words, my mouth is hanging wide open as she goes on. "You shouldn't go near those girls Wayne. Those fucking sluts only want someone to call their ol' man. I pray to God that you are remembering to wrap your shit up tight, so your dick don't fall off. You know better than mixing with that club girl shit. We raised you better than that, didn't we?"

"Jeez Grams, you need to stop talking like that." Rubbing the tears outta my eyes as I stop coughing, "I almost choked to death. You know I would never take a girl like that as an ol' lady. I ain't ready to settle down Grams."

"Why the hell not Wayne? You ain't getting any younger and I need me some great grandbabies."

"Grams, just drop it. You will be the first to know when I find someone ok? It won't be tonight though!"

Sitting for the next hour with Grams, I think again about her words. Me settling down is just not something that I have thought about. Grams does have a point, I am not getting any fucking younger, and if I want to give her some great grandbabies, I might have to start thinking differently about it.

Walking into the clubhouse tonight, I am happy as fuck to know that my prospecting days are done. The vote for Bull and I was held a few weeks back and we were more than thrilled when we got our new patches. Being more than a prospect, and the guys fucking little bitches, has many rewards, one of which is the fucking girls. Bull and I have found ourselves taking some of the club girls together and it is something that gets us off like no other. I have tried my hand at spending time at The Dungeon, but like I told Trip those weeks back, I just had a hard time thinking about the way my dad used to treat Ma. Bull on the other hand, has never had a problem giving pain out at the Dungeon. When I get my dick wet, I just want that, I don't need or want any of that other shit.

Or at least I didn't think that I did.

Glancing around the room again, I see a woman that I have not seen in years. The woman that haunts Gun, and I can't wait to get the story about where she has been, but as I glance at her my eyes stop on the little slice of heaven next to her. I am hard in a second looking over the curves of her body. The outfit that she is wearing is barely there, and it leaves little to the imagination. FUCK she is hot and I will fucking be buried in her tonight if I have anything to say about it.

Drawing my eyes away from her, I look towards Sara again, leaving Bull at the bar I walk over to them. They are at the bar drinking shots with Preach as I slide behind them and throw my arms around Sara in a hug. She relaxes the instant she hears my voice as I growl into her ear, "You're back, huh? It's nice to finally see you again. I had heard as much from some of these motherfuckers." Taking my arms down from around her, I look towards her friend with only lust in my eyes. "Who is this lovely girl here?"

"Country, down boy," she lets out on a giggle. Looking towards her friend, my eyes catch her blush before Sara goes on, "This is my friend Heather. It's nice to see you too. Sorry I haven't stopped by sooner. It's just-" she trails off as Prez, Tank, and Pearl come into the room. All the members and hang arounds shift to look at the trio as the atmosphere changes. Everyone has been looking forward to this since the day they all surrendered to the feelings that they have. I know that the life they lead is not traditional, but it works for them and I couldn't be prouder to call them brothers, or her a sister.

As I settle back with another beer, I can't help myself from staring at Heather. Bull nudges me in the shoulder a few times, trying to speak with me about her, but I can't focus on what he is saying, my gaze is solely focused on her. She is so fucking gorgeous and the curves of her body would feel like heaven beneath me, in-between me and Bull. I see her talking to a few of the brothers and the anger inside of me is off the charts. Why the fuck should I be feeling jealousy I just met this girl, but I can't stop. When I see one of the prospects talking to her, I move towards them quickly before grabbing him roughly by the shoulder, jerking him up and off of the chair he was occupying, and letting him know that she is outta his league and he needs to move the fuck on.

This draws a small laugh from Heather as she looks from me around the room, and when she meets my eyes after trailing them over my body, giving me the eye fucking of the century, I see nothing except lust. Pulling her up outta her seat, I crush my lips to hers and the electricity exchanged is off the wall. We are lost in that kiss for long minutes, before I pull back and see the dark brown of her eyes sparking with fire. I glance down to her lips and see the sides curl up into a smile that is dazzling.

As that same prospect walks past he stops and tries to talk with her, again, which I put to a stop quickly. Heather only laughs as I grab the prospect up by his shoulders, telling him, "Fuck off Prospect. If you come near her again, I will fucking hurt you." Straightening up I lean into her again and am engulfed with pears as I breath in before speaking into her ear, "What's so funny honey? If you were a man, I would lay my hands on you for disrespecting me and laughing at me like that!"

Grabbing my hard cock through my jeans she answers swiftly, "If I were a man, your cock wouldn't be that hard, would it, darlin'?" Pulling back, she glances again towards my crotch and then giggles as she throws her head back laughing. I cannot believe the nerve of this woman. If I were a different man, I would string her up and spank some sense into her. But, the thought of violence mixing with a relationship makes me sick, and I know what I need to do.

I walk away deciding to take a club whore back to my room, instead of this woman who has me wanting to correct her fucking sass. Walking up to the bar I grab two beers and a bottle of Jack from the new prospect before heading towards one of the club girls, Red. Passing Bull on the way, he just shakes his head as I go, knowing what I am thinking before I do, most of the time. Red is sitting with that other girl, what's her fucking name? Fuck it doesn't even matter, but together they should be able to get this fucking hard on I have been sporting since I first saw Heather go away. Grabbing Red up I drag her and her little friend into my room, fucking them both hard, it still takes almost two hours for them to make me come, and it is only with thoughts of that fucking little spitfire on my mind.

FUCK

I knew coming to The Dungeon was probably not the best thing for me to do on a night like tonight, but after meeting that woman at the clubhouse, I couldn't fucking help it. She had me so fucking hard at just the sight of her across the room from me, even after I had those two club whores. Her full hips, that fucking tight ass corset, and the way that her breasts were just sitting there ripe for the picking. FUCK! It took me taking two club whores back to my room and close to two hours of them sucking me off to even get my dick down and as soon as I saw her in the bar area again I was rock fucking hard.

Who the fuck is she? What's her fucking story and why is my cock so fucking hard every time I think about her? I know that she was with Ember and Sara in New Orleans, but don't know much else about her. Why do I even want to know more about her? Maybe after a few nights this weird connection that I am feeling will drown out.

Walking around The Dungeon I see a few scenes playing out, it does nothing for my rock hard cock, thanks yet again to thoughts of Heather. All I can think of is that fucking woman, and as a house sub, Niki comes up to me dropping down to her knees, I think for only moments about taking her to a room and having her deal with my fucking cock, but a scene catches my eye and I leave her kneeling as I walk away towards the scene.

Ember is splayed out on a cross off to one side of the main room and Pearl is working her over with a flogger. I knew that these women had a special bond, but I have never seen it up close and personal. Looking through the crowd I see both of their husbands in the crowd watching intently and I wander over to them. Standing behind them, I continue to watch as Pearl lights up Embers ass with a cane. FUCK that looks like it hurts. The lines that are left on Embers thighs and ass are fucking brutal, she will have those reminders for a long while. As a moan slips from Embers lips around the bright pink ball gag in her mouth, Pearl drops the cane to the floor, and reaches for something, soothing it on over the markings. As she loosens the bindings I hear her lust filled voice only after she licks at Ember's mouth along the ball gag still embedded in her mouth. "On your knees, Sweet thing."

As Ember drops to her knees, the men surrounding me groan out, and I wonder if they have any idea of what is about to come, I sure as shit don't. Looking back towards the scene I see something that I would have never guessed. Pearl loosening the ball gag, and the sound of it popping out of Embers mouth has another groan coming from the crowd. Straddling Embers face with her hands fisting in the red locks, as she rocks her pussy against her face. "Make me come, Sweet thing and I might return the favor. You would like that wouldn't you?"

Only a mumbled, "Yes Ma'am" is heard as the moans from Pearl take over the room. She surely knows how to take control of the room, and really this woman underneath her. Watching the throws of Pearl's orgasm, I know that the show is about to get even more interesting. She orders her little Sweet Thing up onto the table and grabs for not only the vibe but a rather large glass butt plug. I clench at the thought of that large of a plug going into anyone's ass, and Prez must have noticed. Turning back towards me, he grins, "She has taken worse, and enjoys what her Ma'am decides to give to her. You haven't been around to watch them scene before, Country. They are something amazing wouldn't you say?"

As I look back to the scene I see Pearl lubing up both the butt plug as well as Embers asshole. She slowly teases in the plug, and out, and in, and out, until the whole thing is in and a groan spills from Embers lips at the intrusion. When the buzzing starts the look of pleasure that consumes her face, takes away any thought of the pain of the plug in her ass. The lust, longing, and pleasure that I can see in her glassy eyes let me know that she is not only tolerating this, but enjoying it.

"Yes, they sure are something to watch Prez."

And I can't stop myself from thinking how this is different from what my dad used to do to my Ma.

Watching the end of their scene, I move over with their husbands to some couches to the side of the room, and sit for a while drinking another couple beers. As I leave to go home, I find myself hard, thinking again of fucking that woman from the clubhouse. What's her story and why the fuck did she think she could talk to me like that? I need to find out, find her, and bring her to my bed and get myself buried inside her as quick as I can.

CHAPTER
SEVEN

HEATHER

When I walk into the clubhouse with Sara, I don't know what to think. I have never hung around bikers before; I mean shit I watched SOA just like every other red blooded American woman who wanted to see that ass. But, this here was nothing like that show. Of course maybe it was different because this was a wedding, no matter if it was a biker one or not. Right?

We headed for the bar and Sara was instantly pulled into a hug by the bartender, Preach. After a quick shot she was swallowed up in a hug by a big brute of a man. I couldn't help but lose myself in thoughts of him bending me over and fucking me up with the belt, or a cane, or his huge fucking hands. Shaking my head from these thoughts I hear Sara rib him, "Country, down boy." Looking from her to the big brute of a man in front of me the fire I see in his eyes sends jolts of electricity running through me, knowing that my panties are no longer of any use to me. As she puts her hands up to his shirt, a pang of jealousy runs through me as she runs her hands across his broad chest up his collared shirt.

I haven't wanted to be with a man in years, I have only wanted them to give me the pain I seek, and if I gotta give a blowjob that is something I am willing to do, penetration is just too personal. In this moment, however, I can think of nothing that I would like to do more than take this man's cock outta his pants and fucking have it buried deep inside my pussy. Just those thoughts have me near cumming. As Sara draws her hands off of Country we turn and watch as Gun starts the tattoo on Pearl. I have met her a couple times with Sara and Ember and I know that she is a good sort, I am happy that she can find such happiness, but I know it was not meant for me.

Having a few more shots, Sara and I start wandering towards Ember who has caught our eye on the other side of the bar. She and Doc have just found out that they are going to have a baby, and I am glad that this time around he will be there for her. It was hard on her being alone the first time, she needed that man and has blossomed since being back here. Moments later the buzzing from the tattoo gun has stopped and a hard shoulder pushes past me. Seeing Gun grab Sara's hand, he walks her down the hallway towards the back of the clubhouse, and I look to Ember for answers.

After a few words to Doc, she looks at me, and reassures me that Gun would never hurt Sara. That they need to talk things through, and there is nothing we can do about it. I look past her, and see that man, Country at the bar and think again about having him give me something that I have not craved for years. Shaking my head outta the thoughts of him, I turn back to the bar and order another shot and beer, putting some money up on the bar. The young guy behind the bar, looks from me to Doc who is shaking his head, the bartender lets me know that friends aren't to pay.

I take my drink walking over towards an empty table off to the side of the room. As I am sitting there I pull out my cell, checking in with Sophie's babysitter to make sure everything is good. She answers short minutes later, and lets me know Sophie and little Vincent are both sleeping and I should stop worrying and have fun. I think that I agree, only having to wait moments a young guy comes up to me. I see the word prospect on his cut and wonder if he has ever been to The Dungeon. My thoughts instantly go to my last session there with Master Theo. That man handles a whip like none I have ever felt before. The marks that he gave me those weeks ago, have only recently started to fade. Without thinking my hand moves to the underside of my ass and thighs that were so scarred by him.

Listening to this guy try to get into my pants has me wishing he would go the fuck away, and my thoughts are answered quickly as I see Country stalking towards us. As he yanks this kid up outta his seat and away from me by the shoulder, I can't contain the happiness showing on my face and a laugh from tumbling from my lips. Well, at least I won't have to break that young guys heart tonight, not that he had a chance in hell with me, no one does, well almost no one. I feel his eyes on me as I glance around the room before looking back to him. I can't help the eye fucking that I give him, as I look him over before reaching his lust filled eyes. Which I only meet after again trailing them over his body, making sure to get a view of the whole package. Country pulls me up outta my seat, and crushes his lips to mine the second after we make eye contact. The heat that I see as he draws me towards him I have never seen before, even with the Doms that I have had scenes with and especially not with Zack. We are lost in that kiss for long minutes, before he pulls back and I see the brown of his eyes lit up with heat. Looking at him, I can't help the smile that spreads across my face.

As that same prospect walks past he stops and tries to talk with me and I see Country get angry. I laugh nervously at the situation as Country grabs the prospect up by his shoulders, telling him, "Fuck off Prospect. If you come near her again, I will fucking hurt you." The laugh that tumbles from me, is nervous and awkward and still clouded from the kiss that we shared. After straightening up Country leans closer and growls into my ear, with no hint of laughter in his voice. "What's so funny honey? If you were a man, I would lay my hands on you for disrespecting me and laughing at me like that!"

The filter between thought and action is blurred as I grab his hard cock answering, "If I were a man, your cock wouldn't be that hard would it, darlin'?" Pulling back, I glance again towards his crotch and nervously giggle. Not knowing where that came from or why I am feeling quite so nervous I can't stop my head from falling back and the laughter coming.

Where the fuck did that come from? I am not usually that awkward around people, or that disrespectful. I wonder if the attraction I felt the moment I laid eyes on him has anything to do with it. I must have been hoping he was a member of The Dungeon and my blatant disrespect would force his hand to give me the pain that my body is screaming for. As he gets up and stalks away from me, I guess that my assumption was wrong and that me egging him on didn't work like I thought it would. Fuck! I had hoped he would be the one to go a round or two with me tonight, I guess that I will just head to The Dungeon and find someone else to give me what I need.

That man he was next to all night, Bull might be the sort that could cure me of this itch. I have seen him at The Dungeon a time or two, but never to scene. I wonder if he is into pain? If he would be the one to give me what I need? Walking up to the bar, I sit down next to him and slowly turn myself towards him.

"Bull, right?" is all I get out before his crystal blue eyes are on me.

"Don't think about it, Little Thing. You don't get to pit one of us against the other, that will never work out well for you. Go home and take a cold shower, then come talk to us in the morning if you feel the same way." With that he gets up and walks away from the bar and me.

I decide he may be right and going home might be the best bet. Once there however, my need takes over and I wish I would've gone to The Dungeon. Instead I find a small blade and slice thin strips into my thighs. The pain is something and helps to relieve the anxiety, at least for a little while.

The next few weeks go by in much the same manner. Anytime that I go into the clubhouse with Ember or Sara, I find myself getting into an argument with Country or Bull, that is when I run into either of them there. One of those times, I am trying my best to avoid them both, but they decide to try their hand at talking to me together. They approach me as I am playing pool with Ember one night, she quickly realizes what is happening and heads off towards the bar, leaving me alone.

"Spitfire, nice seeing you around tonight." Country says slowly running his fingers down my arm. I wince as he moves over my wrist and him and Bull are on me in a moment. Moving my wrist under the light to look closer at it.

Bull is the first to speak, "Little Thing? What is this? Have you been hurting yourself? I noticed some marks on you the other day when you were here as well."

"I'm just clumsy," shaking their hands off of me, "and this is just another great example of it." Looking from one to the other, I ask, "What did you two come over for? You chased Ember away and we were having fun playing pool. What the fuck do you want with me?" Looking from one to the other annoyed I start to move away, before I am snatched up around the waist by Country.

"No one told you to leave, Spitfire. If we were done with you, we would let you know that you could go."

"If you were done with me, huh? Well, let me tell you two something." Putting my free hand on my hip, I can't stop the venom that the next words leave my mouth with. "There is no man that will ever tell me where to be or when to be there, so both of you can just go," pulling outta his grip, I take a few long strides towards Ember at the bar before turning around and flipping them the bird with both fingers, "and fuck off."

The rest of that night was spent staring daggers at each of them. It lasted for all of an hour, before I had enough and decided sitting at home, would be a better choice. Picking up Sophie from Irene's I am greeted at the back door as I approach.

"Hi Heather, Bull called and said you would be coming. Let me go grab Sophie for you and help you get her settled in."

Putting a hand on her shoulder, I stop her from turning and make my way over to the couch. Picking up Soph, I walk past Irene, stopping to kiss her on the cheek and thank her again for watching my girl. Awkwardly unlocking the door, I finally get Soph to her room, putting her down softly onto the bed.

As the days pass, things are as tense between us as they have been between Sara and Gun. When I was at home with Sophie the other day, Gun came over to talk with me. Awkward is not even how I would begin to describe the exchange that happened between us.

Seeing him across the way out on Irene's porch with her, I don't pay much attention. In the few weeks that I have been here, I have seen him a few times. We have never been introduced, but Sara cannot help to talk about the man she loves, even after all this time. As I go about enjoying this beautiful day with Sophie playing out in the yard, I notice him moving towards me instantly. Looking towards Irene I see her smile and nod, before addressing him.

"You must be Gun," comes out as he stops a few feet from me. Before he can answer Sophie has come bounding over and is rambling on and on.

"Mom, is this Gun? The guy that Auntie Sara is always talking about?" I chuckle at her beautiful naivety and security in talking with this man that is big, covered in tattoos, menacing, and just plain scary to any soul that sees him.

Before I can answer Gun begins, "Yes, I am Gun. Your auntie talks about me?" he says looking first at Sophie then towards me.

Rolling my eyes at his digging, I know that this is a fishing trip if I ever saw one. "Why did you come over here, Gun?" Looking between him and back towards Irene, who has not moved from the swing on her porch, "I thought like the other afternoons you have spent with Irene you would stay over there for your visit. What brought you over here anyway? You know Sara is at work. Right?"

"I do know that she is not here. I just heard from Irene how you helped Ember out when she got to New Orleans and wanted to make sure that I thanked you for that. I am not sure what, if anything Doc knows about those times, but I am sure that he would also like to show his appreciation for what help you gave to his ol' lady."

"Hmm, yes well, I was raised to always help those in need and that is what I did." Not knowing what his end game is I think it better if he gets on back over to Irene's before this exchange goes somewhere it needs not go. "Why don't you skedaddle back over to Irene's house now, or better yet leave because Sara will be home soon. She sure as hell doesn't need to see you here or sniffing around over there either it's bad enough she will hear all about it from Soph as soon as she gets home."

Looking at me like I just slapped his face, the volume of his voice drops and the Dom that I have seen only a few times from the shadows at The Dungeon steps in. "What are you talking about? Sniffing around?"

Being thankful that this man is not mine, I take a deep breath to steady myself as I begin, "I can only imagine what the two of you were like when you were together, probably hornier than a two peckered owl." Drawing in another deep breath I meet his eyes before continuing, "What I do know is that the feelings you have for each other are not in the past and y'all need to figure it out. The longer you keep up with these games, the less time you will have with each other." Instantly feeling regret on the way that I have been letting the attraction between Country and I go on makes me question if I am the right person to be giving advice.

He looks so pissed off as he answers, and I am again reminded of the man that I have seen only glimpses of at The Dungeon. "I didn't come here sniffing after Sara like a horny owl. I am taking care of Irene, like I have done the past five years that she has been gone. Don't think that just because she has finally made her way home that I will stop doing what I promised to do. Watching out for Irene became my job when she ran away, and I have no intention of stopping."

Seeing the anger, hurt, and love in those eyes has me wishing that the two of them would talk this shit out. They are both so hurt and once they work through this shit both of their lives will be better. Just from that one interaction with Gun and the stories I have heard from Sara, I know that they are everything to each other and the sooner they give in the better. I know exactly the feelings they bring out in each other though, when Country or his friend approaches me, I can't help the shit I say to them. I can't believe either of them is even still trying to be nice to me, I have been nothing but sarcastic as fuck to each of them. I honestly have not been trying to act that way, it's like anytime one of them is near me the brain to mouth filter I have fails. Last week was the worst of it. I came in with Sara and we were both buzzed up, I shouldn't have done what I did, but I couldn't help it, my inhibitions were gone.

On Saturday, as we walked through the clubhouse, I see Country in a second, with one of the club whores on his lap. I got so fucking pissed just like I do whenever he is talking to or touching another woman. Sara and Ember have both picked up on my erratic behavior around him. They both love telling me that I am acting that way because I like him, and that scares me even more. Looking towards him again, Sara tries to stop me, but I just can't stop myself. I walk up to him, grabbing the girl off of him before tugging him up outta his seat and down the hall towards the guy's rooms.

Country didn't say anything as I tugged him into his room, which I was in that once to change my clothing. Ugh, my stalker tendencies have been in full force these last few weeks watching his every move. The night that I made a mess on my shirt and needed to use his room to change, helped me know which room was his. I sink down to my knees pausing at how natural, pleasing, and safe it feels in front of this man. Grabbing for the buckle of his belt with no other thoughts than his cock in my mouth I pull his dick free. Looking up at him from my spot on the floor, I see the hunger in his eyes and can't help the moan that escapes my lips as I pull his cock free from his jeans.

Licking my lips, I hear a groan from him before my lips wrap around his cock and I slowly swallow it all. Seeing the door behind us open, I watch as Bull's head peeks around it, before his whole body soon stands in the opening. Watching the fire burn in his eyes as I swallow his friend's cock, has me reaching a hand towards my pussy. As I pick up the pace, I feel Country's hands tangle in my hair and he quickly takes control of the rhythm, forcing his cock further and further into my throat. Seeing Bull stroking his cock while watching me blow his friend, has me nearing an orgasm. Gagging a few times on his cock has tears falling from my eyes, and my heartbeat racing. Seeing Bull move slightly, I notice his face as he comes onto his hand, before he turns and walks out shutting the door quietly behind himself. I am not even sure if Country knows that he was in here, but that shit was hot as fuck. Continuing taking turns swallowing him and stroking him it is not long before I start to feel his balls tighten up. He reaches down under my arms and yanks me up, not wanting to finish in my mouth. Tossing me towards the bed, he climbs on top of me and pushes up my skirt. The next thing I know, my panties are being ripped from my body and he sinks into me.

Screaming out in pain, it rivals the night I lost my cherry, there is pleasure mixed with pain, in those first moments. His first thrust into me commanding an orgasm to scream free from my body. Fuck, no sex since Sophie came does something to a girl I guess. Like he can read my thoughts, he stills inside of me, his eyes meet mine and the electricity that goes between us, frightens me. Leaning into me, he takes my mouth with his own and kisses the breath out of me. I am lost in the feelings of him fucking me, until my orgasm is quickly wrung from my body. After a few more strokes, he pushes me over the edge again, and follows me over.

Pulling away from me, Country walks into the attached bathroom, shutting the door behind himself. Feeling like utter and complete used up trash, I quickly adjust my clothing and head out the door, in the hall I make my way right past a grinning Bull, and a blush heats my cheeks. Not looking back, I let Sara know I am leaving and head to the only place that will make this shame I feel from this fucking one night stand better.

I have been to The Dungeon more than usual since I met him and that's where I find myself heading tonight as soon as I get outta the clubhouse. Needing to get the thoughts of them to subside, because the pain from my new tattoo and piercing is not cutting it any longer. Pulling into the lot, I glance around and see that it is still not too busy, but

I know a lot of the people from the clubhouse will be heading over here shortly and I would like to be gone before then. I grab my bag of club wear outta the trunk and head inside. Greeting Shadow at the back door, I inquire about the Doms that are here tonight. He mentions Master Theo and I know that he is just the sort of pain that I am craving tonight. Walking into the locker room, I find Peach fixing her makeup in the mirror.

"Hey Peach." Comes out a lot louder than I meant it too, startling her to the point that her eye liner slips outta her grip. "Oh fuck, sorry Peach, I didn't mean to startle you." Looking up to me in the mirror, I notice that her eyes are puffy and it looks like she has been crying. Dropping my bag, I rush over to her and throw my arms around her. "What's wrong luv? Is it a man? Do you need me to go get someone? Shadow is by the door."

"Shadow? No, I'm fine. It is just that-" Shaking her head she stares off for long moments before going on. "Harold, my step-father reached out to me and it just-" Losing herself again, I give her a small squeeze which brings her right back to her story, "he used to abuse me and I haven't heard from him in years. I didn't think he would be able to find me so I" she is cut off by the sobs that start. I get up to my feet and head towards the door, looking over my shoulder I say, "I'll go grab Shadow and he will be able to-"

Cutting me off, she wipes at the tears that have been falling down. "No, no please don't. I will be fine in a few minutes." Turning to look at me her eyes plead with me to leave it be.

"Okay, but if you need to talk about anything you know that I am here for you, whenever you need."

"Thanks, Heather." Swiping at the last tears, she wipes away the makeup and starts again as I get dressed. Looking towards Peach as I step towards the door, she gives a shy smile and nods her head in approval at me before I walk out into the club.

Seeing Master Theo at the bar, I walk confidently towards him. As if he senses me behind him, he turns slowly and the grin on his face spreads as recognition hits, letting me know that this sadist is only too happy to give me what I long for.

"Precious, you didn't have enough last time? Would you like for me to have another go with you?"

"Yes please, Theo. I would love to have a session with you tonight." Looking around the area, "If you are free that is?"

"For you Precious, I can make time. The main room is getting used by Master Markus's Pet tonight, so if you don't mind we will have to use one of the private rooms?"

Stilling at the thought of not being watched, or having someone close by if I need help has me double guessing this idea. But, Theo must read the fear in my face, and instantly steps closer to me, gently placing a hand on my arm.

"Nothing will happen that you do not want to happen. I know how you feel about sex Heather, and just like the last time we have sessioned, we will follow the same limits we have set previously. No penetration, safewords are red, yellow, and green as always."

Looking me over, from head to toe, he leans in before speaking again. "I can't believe after that last session you are coming back for more, you sure are one hell of a pain slut I didn't go easy on you last time and tonight will be no different. Is that what you would like?"

"Yes, Theo, that is what I want. Give it your best shot. I know that everyone here, just like back at Club Coquin, tries to bring the pain slut to her knees."

"That's where you came from huh? New Orleans is surely a city for sin."

Leading me away from the bar, he talks with one of the floor monitors before we are assigned a room. We walk slowly down the hall stopping at the second door on the left. The room that I've nicknamed the hot seat because it has some of the most painful toys in it that I have ever experienced. Taking a deep breath in front of the door, I steady the pounding of my heart as I think about what has caused me to this point again. Instead of my usual thoughts, of how the pain calms me, the only thought that I have is of Country. His face is all I see and I pass over the threshold and enter "The Hot Seat."

After about an hour, Theo has taken me down off of the cross and is rubbing something into the fresh strips that he has laid out on my skin. I fall hard as I come down from the endorphins that are coursing through my body. Theo is there the entire time, cooing words into my ear, but I wish he was someone else. At that, I lie to him and let him believe that I am fine, when in reality I am anything but.

"Theo, thank you again for the session. I am fine, and would love just a few minutes alone to myself, if possible?"

"Precious are you sure? You just flew not but ten minutes ago, you have to be crashing hard, and you know I should be here to watch over you."

Grabbing at my chin, I slink away from him and look directly into his eyes, as I let him know, "I am fine Theo, and would like it if you would just leave."

Nodding his head, he moves towards his shirt and shrugs it on before heading to the door. When I hear the door close behind him, my head drops to the pillow and the cry that rips through me has nothing to do with the pain on my skin, but the pain I feel for letting myself get caught up again.

As I cry my thoughts drift to the man that I fucked only a few short hours ago. He is someone that I could see myself getting attached to real quick, and that's a problem for me. I just dragged him into his fucking room tonight and sank down to my knees like he was something to me. I promised myself when I left Zack that I would never get involved again.

Country is definitely someone that I could see myself falling for, and I think that is why I can't seem to keep my shit together around him. And what the fuck was that shit with Bull? Is that something that they do? I know that

Pearl has two husbands and shit, but that is definitely some weird ass shit. The feelings that I find myself with are why I can't stop myself from pushing Country away every chance I get even though I really and truly don't want to. I mean, fuck, I don't want to be a bitch, it just sort of comes out when I am near him, either of them really.

As I get redressed and leave the room, I walk down the hall towards the main entrance. There is a small limp as I go, the pain searing through my thighs, ass, and back is torturing my movements. As I clear the hallway and take a few steps into the main room, I take in the people that have come since I went into the room with Theo. As I glance around the room, I see no one and make it only a few steps, before I am hoisted up off the ground and dragged back towards the hallway. I struggle in muscled arms before a door is opened and I am placed on a bed. When I realize who has snatched me up, I relax and am looking into eyes that burn with anger, lust, and if I didn't know better, I would say love.

FUCK I am in more trouble than I thought.

CHAPTER EIGHT

COUNTRY

For the last few weeks, each time I am in the clubhouse and Heather is there the tension between us is palpable, to say the least. The way that she acts around me and Bull, has me questioning if there is something wrong with her. She is always nervous around me and I try to be cool with her but it's kinda fucking weird how awkward she is. If I didn't know better I would say that the attraction between us scares her, but she has a fucking kid, so I know that she has been around the block a time or two.

For fucks sake last week I ran into her with Sara at the clubhouse and she spilt her drink when I bumped into her, by accident might I add, up at the bar. Like literally all over herself, she started laughing nervously and turned the brightest shade of red. I let her use my room to change into some clothes that she borrowed from Sara and we didn't talk much for the rest of the night. After I made my way to my room later, I could smell her pear perfume and my cock started to throb in a second. The thought of going to get a club girl to take care of the problem didn't even cross my mind. It hasn't, since that first night when I met Heather. I have been jerking off to thoughts of her, and I know that I am only biding time, until she and I get together on this fucking attraction we have between us. I just need her to relax enough around me to be comfortable before I make my fucking move.

Tonight has lead me to one decision and one decision alone. She will be mine I just need to get her through this fucking awkwardness between us before that can happen. Bull and I have talked a few times, and we have come to an understanding. If she can find it in herself to be with the both of us, that is something that we will try to make happen.

I haven't touched one of the club girls since that first night that we met. Until tonight that is. Red, wouldn't leave me alone all night and during the moments that she fell in my lap, before my Spitfire came and dragged her off me, I got a glimpse into Heather's real feelings. Seeing the anger in her eyes as she approaches us, my cock is fucking hard the instant I see her acting so possessive.

We don't speak as I get hauled down the hall towards my room. As we walk through the door of my room, she is dropping to her knees instantly. Seeing her there, kneeling for me, has my mind racing to all the subs I have seen do it before. None of them have gotten close to the reaction from my cock as this fucking spitfire is getting now. My cock is straining already as she reaches for the buckle on my belt, she runs her tongue across her lips looking up at me with such lust and longing in her eyes. Yanking my cock free from my pants, as soon as her hand touches the flesh of my shaft, I groan drawing her eyes back up to meet mine. Impaling her mouth on my cock, is the sweetest fucking feeling, and I know instantly that she was meant for me. As her pace picks up, I can't stop myself from wrapping my hands into her hair, taking control of this, of us. Shoving my cock deep inside of her mouth I groan again as I feel her throat constrict around my cock. As she swallows me down, I am fucking amazed at the feelings of her mouth surrounding me, and as I look down at her I fucking almost lose it.

Gagging a few times on my cock has tears falling from her eyes, almost pushing me over again. That's when I notice her eyes on the door and I glance towards the door. Seeing Bull there doesn't surprise me in the least. She's struggling to deal with me alone, I don't know if there is a chance in hell that we both have a shot. I stop myself from cumming before reaching down to tug her up, throwing her onto the bed, I don't waste time losing any of my clothing. Before I sink into her, I look again to the door, but notice he is gone. Looking back towards Heather, I find myself pushing up her skirt as I sink into her without pause. The scream of pain that rips through her has me stopping quickly, which doesn't stop her cunt from tightening down on my cock in an orgasm. Looking into her eyes, the electricity that bounces between us, lets me know that my feelings for her, for us are not one sided.

Dropping my mouth down to hers, consuming her with a kiss, I don't wait long before picking up the pace of my strokes. Pulling my cock outta her body almost the whole way, my head moves away from her as I slowly sink back in drawing another moan from her lips. Looking down towards where we are joined, I get lost in watching my cock slide into her cunt and back out. After a few more strokes, I feel her legs start to shake and the walls of her cunt start to strangle my cock for the second time, as I chase my own orgasm, burying myself deep inside of her.

After a few long moments buried deep inside of her, I pull away slowly, heading towards the bathroom. Opening the door, I hear it bounce against the wall before it shuts behind me, as I walk towards the sink to clean myself up. Pausing as I realize I didn't wear a condom tonight with her, FUCK. She is mine and I shouldn't be putting her at risk, especially since we haven't spoken about birth control or even had the tests done to make sure each of us is clean. Grabbing the wash cloth up off the cupboard, I turn on the water, letting it warm up before washing myself off, and cleaning the cloth before turning to head back to the bed and my woman. Opening the door back-up, I take two steps before I notice that Heather is no longer in my bed. Glancing around the room, it takes me a few seconds before I realize that she fucking walked, nah fuck that, ran out on me. Adjusting my clothing I walk out into the main room, looking for that little Spitfire that I am about to lay into. Not seeing her, I notice Sara and head over to her.

"Where did she go, Sara?" I harshly spit out at her.

"Don't speak to me that way, Country. You may be pissed off about something," wiggling her eyebrow at me, "or someone. But you will not be disrespecting me like that."

Looking through the room, I notice her eyes move to the door and guess were my little Spitfire has gone. "She ran didn't she?"

"You two need to talk about this, Country. I know that you have been patient and that she acts like a fucking lunatic around you, but that isn't her. You both need to just sit down and work through your shit."

Grunting towards her, I move back to my room stopping for a moment as I move past Bull in the hall. "Don't think I didn't see you in there, Bull, I told you this shit wasn't for you. I don't think that this one is for sharing. She can barely handle the feelings that I have for her before running outta the fucking door, who knows what will happen if you were in the fucking mix."

"You so sure about that Country, her eyes sang a different tune while you were fucking her throat. And her hand was buried in her pussy, getting herself off."

Not knowing what to think I shove past him, slamming the door behind myself as I enter my room. Moving towards the bed, I catch a smell of her perfume and find myself hard. Grabbing myself, I tighten my hand down on my cock trying to relieve some of the tension. Knowing that staying here in my room tonight, is not something that I am going to be comfortable with, I grab my bag and head out the door, to the one place I can lose myself in a crowd and have a few drinks, trying to relieve the war that I find within myself.

Passing Bull again on my way outta my room, I nod my head at him, "Come on, lets head over to The Dungeon. I can't be in there thinking about this shit with her, having her fucking smell still in my room."

Bull doesn't hesitate to fall in step behind me. I know that he has an interest in Heather and that we have had women together before, but I really don't know if she would be able to handle it. She is fighting being with me so much, and to try and do something so unusual as having both of us be with her, might force her to run away.

The drive over goes quick, and as I am sitting at the bar taking a slug from my beer, I look around to these people that surround me. Seeing Theo walking down the hall, I wonder who the unlucky person to be on the receiving end of him was tonight. My thoughts drift to the hips and thighs of the woman I was buried inside only hours ago, who ran as soon as she could. Like I conjured her with my thoughts, she comes walking down the hallway towards the main room. My dick is instantly hard, seeing her in a tight leather skirt and bra. She walks past slowly without noticing us, and as she passes I catch the little limp in her step and hear a groan spilling from her lips. I crank my neck around wondering what has her moving in such a way, when I notice the welts on her creamy thighs and put two and two together.

Getting up from my seat I move quickly towards her. Grabbing her up off of the ground, I turn us around and walk directly back down the hallway she had come from. Nodding my head at the floor monitor he lets me know that the last door on the right is open. I push open the door as Heather struggles against me. I think better of tossing her onto the bed, and as gently as possible with her struggling against me I put her onto the bed, never taking my hands off of her.

"What the fuck?" She looks up into my eyes before registering who I am. As recognition hits, she relaxes in my grip, "Country, what are you doing?"

"I'm trying my best not to go after Theo and put him down, for touching what is mine. Bringing you in here was the first thought I had to stop myself from that, so I did it." Running a hand through my hair I move closer to her rolling her momentarily onto her side, before running my hand over her thigh where the welts are now raging, "That is who did this to you right?"

"Country, it is none of your business what I fucking do with my life. Who the fuck do you think you are? I only met you a few weeks ago and every time I am around you I fucking lose it. You think that you have the right to tell me what the fuck I can do? Or who the fuck I can have sex with? Just because I made the mistake of letting you fuck me tonight, doesn't mean shit. You were the one who was outta the bed, before your cum stopped leaking outta me. Who do you think you are trying to tell me what the fuck to do? My fucking Master or some shit?" she tries pushing me off of the bed with no luck.

I look up to her eyes, and laugh at the anger I see there. I am so fucking hard it hurts and she is so fucking angry. I can't explain why these two shouldn't fucking mix between us, but they do and the fire they are stirring in me is something that doesn't need any stoking. All the years I saw my father beating on my ma I should not get aroused by my fucking Spitfire acting like this. Especially doing what I know she let that man do to her and the marks that still mark her body. But, I fucking am aroused and I'm betting by the smells coming off of her, so is she.

Moving closer again, I run a hand up her stomach to her breast, hearing the hitch in her breathing has me thinking that I am not the only one that wants this, again. "You let him put his hands on you like this, Spitfire?"

Slowly she shakes outta her own thoughts, and answers, "It's none of your business, Country."

Grabbing her up roughly, I spit out, "Fuck yes it is, Spitfire. You. Are. Mine. I was buried inside of you not even three hours ago and now you are here letting that fucker, do the same? Fucking you tonight was something I have been wanting since the moment I first saw you. Then, you just fucking run to another man before I could even get back to clean you up and bury myself inside of you again?"

Rolling her eyes at me, I lunge even closer towards her leaving no room separating us, attacking her mouth with my own. Forcing her back on the bed, I hear the hiss and don't care one bit about the marks on her body that have caused it. She shouldn't have let him touch what is mine, she will learn in time, that all of her belongs to me, and me alone.

Pulling back slightly her lips follow mine as I ask, "Did he touch you?" Licking her lips, I go on, "Did he touch what is mine?" Moving my head slowly to her neck, I nip at her before licking and kissing away the pain, "Did he fuck you?" Pulling back sharply I make sure to have her eyes on mine before I finish my thought," Because if he did, I will fucking put him down, like the dog that he is."

"What?" shaking herself out of the fog of lust that has crept over not only her, "No, what? No we didn't fuck, he didn't fucking touch me like that, he never does, none of them ever do, they know better than that. No one ever touches me like that." Dropping her eyes from my own, she shakes her head from side to side. "Only you."

"Don't fucking lie to me Spitfire, I can see his marks on you." Grabbing at her chin, I tilt her head up to meet my eyes, "Did you kneel for him, like you did for me not even three hours ago?" Shaking her head, she tries to pull away, but I hold tight as I complete my thoughts, "He touched you I know that much. If he put his dick anywhere near you I will fucking end him, though. I will end him if he even fucking thought about it. You. Are. Mine."

"It's not about sex, Country, not with them." Dropping her eyes from mine, she tries again to pull away, but I hold her closer to me as she goes on, "It is only about the pain, I need it. Fuck, tonight is the first time I thought about sex since before I had Sophie six years ago." Glancing towards me, she blushes deeply then adds, "well since the first time I met you, that is."

Licking her lips, draws my thoughts to being buried inside of her again. Then, the first words register with me and I am taken back as the shock of her words strike me like a blow to the face. "What do you mean that you need the pain?" I see her flinch as I shout at her, spinning her around and pointing to the marks that are now on her flesh, "NO ONE FUCKING NEEDS PAIN LIKE THAT HEATHER!"

CHAPTER NINE

HEATHER

When Country dragged me through The Dungeon like that I was instantly snapped outta the anxiety I was feeling from my session with Theo. I didn't want to run off from The clubhouse, but the way that Country just walked into the bathroom leaving me alone, had me so fucking scared that I had made a horrible mistake. As soon as he took control of me, when he demanded that I do what he say and that I belonged to him, I felt something that I have never felt before, and that scares me even more. In the moments that passed between us after he yelled about not needing pain, my mind is going a mile a minute trying to think up a way to explain my needs to him.

Before I am able to get my thoughts together, he is on top of me. Pushing the short leather skirt up and over my hips, ripping the soaked panties off of my body. Unbuckling his belt, pulling it through his pants and using it to tie my hands to the headboard, before freeing his cock, I find him flipping me over as his arm comes under my waist and he pulls me up onto my hands and knees. Gasping for breath, I turn my head to the side, as I notice Bull standing just inside of the door. Feeling myself close to cumming again at the thought of him watching us, I am pushed over as Country slams deep inside of me. My eyes don't leave

Bulls as Country rakes his fingernails along the welts that have been forming on my thighs, ass, and back, growling into my ear. "This is the last time, I am not there to witness marks being put on this flesh Spitfire, or you will not enjoy the consequences." Moving a hand to my neck, he squeezes tightly before finishing his thought, ramming into me after each word. "YOU. ARE. MINE. NOTHING. COMES. BETWEEN. ME. AND. WHAT. IS. MINE. NOTHING." With that, I lose my breath for a brief second and drop my eyes from Bulls as they fall shut before the most intense orgasm takes over my body, and I fly like I never have before.

Not knowing how much time has passed, I wake up cradled into Country's lap wrapped in blankets. Noticing me stirring, he reaches to the side table grabbing some chocolate and water up off of the table. Holding the piece of chocolate to my lips, I spread them open as he places it into my mouth. I lose myself as I taste not only the sweet but I find myself lucky enough to still have his fingers inside of my mouth. Licking and sucking on them, I feel his cock hardening against my ass as a moan leaves his lips. Glancing around I don't see Bull and wonder if he was nothing more than a figment of my imagination.

Sliding his fingers outta my mouth, a chuckle leaves him before I hear the reprimand leaving his mouth. "Spitfire, that is enough of that. You are insatiable and I will do my best to keep your desires at bay, but we need to discuss a few things and set some fucking rules before I lose myself to you again. I was caught up in The clubhouse by you dragging me into my room, and then was so pissed to find you gone. Then I get here and within a short time, I am buried inside of you again. Let's get ourselves dressed and we can go to my house and talk. Work out the ins and outs of this shit, and figure out how this ol' lady shit is gonna work."

Looking up at him, the glow from the orgasm fades quickly as his words sink in. "Country, I can't go home with you. I gotta get home to Sophie, I can't leave her with Irene overnight. Just because we have had sex a couple times today, doesn't mean that we need to be in a relationship or something like that. I don't expect that from you, Country, and I am pretty sure that being your ol' lady is not something that I would do well with." Sitting up I am quickly met with resistance as I try to move away from him to the edge of the bed. "I will just get ready and head home, we'll see each other when we see each other."

Dropping his arms off of my body he lets out a groan as I make quick work of escaping off the bed. "Country, not three months ago we didn't even know each other. Two months ago we had only just met and I couldn't keep myself from losing all conscious thought around you. Now today we have fucked twice, without protection might I add, and all of a sudden you think that I'm your ol' lady and that we need to be building a future together? I don't fucking think so, you can't be the man I need, you can't give me what I need, Country."

"You know what, if you're gonna fight it this much Heather, then I know that this shit between us must mean more to me than it does to you. I have waited since the first night I saw you to be buried deep inside you and I had guessed that you felt the same. If you don't feel that though, I'm not gonna chase after you like some lost puppy dog." Scrubbing a hand over his face, he locks eyes with me before nodding towards the door, "Don't let that get stuck up your ass on the way out Spitfire." Throwing himself off of the bed, he heads towards the door to the bathroom, grabbing his clothing up as he goes. "You know what, you are probably right, I can't handle all the crazy that you are throwing off. Maybe it is best that you let some sick fuck whip your ass and get off on your pain."

He slams the door shut as I pick my jaw up off the floor and know that I just fucked up my chance with this man. The only man that I have ever felt this way about, the first man I have thought about having a meaningful future with since Zack. I should head into the bathroom right now and drop to my knees and beg forgiveness, but that just isn't gonna happen- I have already been on my knees twice for him today, and that was two times too many. I thought I would kneel for no one and he has me doing it twice today already. That thought makes my feet move closer to the door until my hand rests on the handle for long moments until I make, what feels like might be the hardest decision of my life. Turning the knob, I move through the door, and head through the club to my car. Passing by Bull on my way out the door, he grabs for my arm stopping me in my tracks.

"Heather, you are going about this with him the wrong way. You should have never been here tonight after what happened between us," shaking his head, "no between the two of you tonight. I'm not sure what happened after I left that room but it could not have been bad enough to force your hand to come here, like this. I have seen you here before, and never told Country about it." Reaching towards me I try to step back but I'm greeted with the wall, "Your need for pain is something that I find absolutely amazing, and if pain is something so dear to you, then you need to talk to Country about that, don't just run from his bed to come here and take another man into a room. That shit wouldn't fly with me and it sure as fuck won't fly with Country."

Pulling away from him I find myself enraged at his words. "Why are you talking like you and I have anything between us, Bull? You came in tonight and watched me give him a blow job and then just now in there, you watched him fuck me. That's all."

"You are wrong there Little Spitfire. I saw a gorgeous woman give herself up to a man that she has been fighting for a long while. Then submit even further by allowing me to watch as she pleased that man, pleasing me in turn. I am not sure how much you have actually seen or heard while you have been at the clubhouse or even at The Dungeon, but Country and I have been brothers for a lot longer than we have been in this MC and in more ways than just through this MC. Do yourself a favor and just be honest with him, with me, and with yourself about what you truly want, what you need, and what you desire."

Moving away from me slowly, I am left in shock at the words that he has spoken to me. Not only did I have that shit go on with Country and him at the clubhouse tonight, but now having to deal with them both here as well. It's too fucking much, and why does he think that he knows what I am thinking and feeling? I have only spoken to that man two or three times since I met him, and none of those conversations were more than a hey what's up.

UGH! Fucking men.

Reaching Sara's, no our home, about a half an hour later, I head over to Irene's to pick Sophie up. Noticing a motorcycle parked on the street in front of Irene's I walk a few steps closer to the street and notice that it looks a lot like the one that I have seen Preach on the couple of times I have seen the men all riding together. Walking in the front door, I head straight to the couch, grabbing Sophie up and off of it spinning back towards the door. Seeing a bottle of Jack on the kitchen island and two glasses on the table next to it has me wondering if Irene had company tonight, maybe that was Preach's bike that I saw outside. I'll have to talk to her about it tomorrow when I see her. I know that Gun has been keeping an eye on her during the years that Sara has been gone, but he was with Sara last night and I am pretty sure that they didn't come over here for a night cap.

I don't see Irene for a few days, and when I do finally catch up with her I am sure to bring up the two glasses that were on her table that night.

"Irene, thanks again for watching Sophie the other night. I really do wish you would take some money."

Cutting me off abruptly she answers harshly, "No Heather, you know better than that. You helped my girls out greatly in New Orleans and I will do what I can to help repay that. Anything that you need, I will be here to help."

Smiling at her grandmotherly way, I walk to her and throw my arms around her. As I hug her to myself I smell something that is not Irene's usual smell, and instantly realize what must have been going on. Pulling back from her, I look into her eyes as recognition passes between us. "Irene, he was here that night wasn't he?"

Pulling away from her, I move towards her room, and she yells out, "Don't you dare, little Girl. My personal life has nothing to do with you. If I have a male visitor it is not for you or Sara, or anyone to judge or know. So, put your mind somewhere else and leave it be. DO. YOU. HEAR. ME?"

Laughing, I move back towards her and again throw my arms around her, "I love you Irene and whatever you do is your business," Pulling back slightly I look into her eyes as I ask a question that I shouldn't. "I was just curious if it was Preach's bike that I saw here that night?" Seeing her eyes flash with guilt, I see in a moment the answer she will never give. I am happy to know that she is happy, but sad that she doesn't feel like she can share that happiness with me, I wonder if Sara or Gun have any idea.

Like she is reading my thoughts, she answers, "They don't know, no one does. Please keep it that way, Little Girl. We cannot keep away from each other it seems, and I am not sure if that is something that we want the world to know. When my Earl was still around we fought so hard against the feelings we had, with him gone now, things have changed, Little Girl." The frown she had thinking of her late husband, leaves the instant her mind moves on to Preach, and I am happy knowing that she has found something good.

Two weeks have passed and I haven't gone to the clubhouse since the night that we had sex. I just don't want to run into Country or Bull and have either one of them be as weird and awkward as I think I would be around them. I fucked Country in his room, without a word between us while getting off on Bull watching what was happening. Who the fuck does that? What the fuck is wrong with me? Then I let him take me again at The Dungeon, with only a fight to follow that as well. Why couldn't I just be nice to him? Be a normal fucking person around him? Treat him the way that I truly feel about him inside?

I have thought about his cock inside of me each night as I have laid in bed, and found my fingers trailing towards my pussy. I have dreamt of him spanking my ass, paddling my ass raw, and whipping my thighs, ass, and back bloody. He is not that man. I have seen Country these last few weeks at The Dungeon, I have watched him from the shadows. He doesn't even watch any of the pain sluts or the scenes that they are in. The times he is there when I am, he tends to watch the tamer scenes and that's how I know he will never be able to handle my special brand of fucked up.

That first week I was sore from his fucking of me, enough so that even peeing hurt. He really worked me over that night, and I can't even imagine what it would be like if we were together on a long term basis. I would need fucking ice packs or something like that. The ache that I felt for that first week, not only from Country but from the stings of the cane that Theo had used on me, helped to calm my racing mind, a little at least. When I would find myself getting anxious or thinking too long about Country, I would run my fingers roughly over the scars. I reinjured one of them from my "ministrations" and it is only now starting to scab over, I hope the anxiousness keeps at bay so I don't reinjure myself.

CHAPTER
TEN

COUNTRY

Two long weeks, since I left her in that room at The Dungeon, and she is avoiding the clubhouse and The Dungeon like the fucking plague. I know the shit I yelled at her, I had no right to say but she gets under my skin, and I can't control what comes outta my mouth. Not that I haven't seen her during that time, I sure as fuck have gone past the house and watched her. Bull and I have taken turns for fucks sake. I know that she will come around in time, but I want to make sure that if she needs pain like she told me that night, I will sure as fuck be the one to decide when and where she gets it. I have noticed the marks on her thighs the few times I have seen her outside, and noticed the scars seem fresh, wondering what she has been doing to herself I have to hold back my thoughts of going to her.

Giving myself only two more days before I go to her, I walk into the clubhouse and have a seat next to Prez and Tank. Prez looks towards me, nodding his head before saying, "Brother, it's good to see you here tonight." Taking a swig from his beers, he motions to the prospect for two more. "Thanks for being there for us these last few weeks. I think things are finally starting to settle down, but I never know for sure and it's good to know that we have brothers watching our backs." Nodding my head, he smiles as he goes on, "I have watched how well you have taken to being a member, and I wanted to tell you I couldn't be prouder." Clapping me on the shoulder he goes on, "We have something special planned coming up and we were wondering if you would be able to help out."

"Yeah, whatever it is Prez, you know I'll help out however I can." Taking a long swig from my beer, I look back towards him, "What's up?"

"I knew we could count on you. Doc will talk to you more about it when you see him, but he is surprising Ember with a wedding on Valentine's Day and I was hoping that you and your little Spitfire would be willing to help out."

Shaking my head, "She is not my Spitfire, Prez. She ran quicker than a jack rabbit being chased by a hound that night from The Dungeon, she wants nothing to do with me." The laughs coming from both Prez and Tank has me snapping my eyes to them. "What the fuck are you two laughing about?"

Tank is the first to answer, "We have seen it in each of ourselves, as well as Gun, Doc, Shadow, and even recently with Preach. That little Spitfire has you, just as our Pearl has us- you and her can fight it all you want, but in the end, if you are smart, you will find your way to each other."

Clapping Tank on the shoulder, Prez nods in agreement, adding "So right, brother, so right. If we would not have admitted our feelings for our little pet, we would not be as happy as we find ourselves now. We have Rebel, Iris, Rose, and our Pearl," smiling wide he finishes his thought, "Our lives have never been better. You will get there as well brother."

"Of course Prez. Congrats to you and Tank by the way. I don't know if I ever really got the chance to tell you that after the wedding and all that. It got kinda crazy around here and then at The Dungeon." Looking towards their bride, I smile and add, "You are both lucky sons of bitches."

"That we are Country. That we are." Looking towards his wife, who is across the room playing pool, Prez gets up and heads over by her, taking her mouth with his own. As I look around from Pearl, I see Heather outta the corner of my eye. She is finally here, and I will not waste this opportunity with her. Nodding towards us I head for her moving fast. Approaching her, I make sure to leave her no escape route as I corner her behind the pool table.

Leaning in close, I smell the pears and find myself hard, not unusual in her presence even though it has been two weeks since I have been this close to her. Reaching for her hand, I move my eyes slowly over the outfit she is wearing and growl into her ear, "Did you wear this to get a rise outta me, Spitfire?"

"Country, back up a bit. I'm here playing pool with Pearl and I-" she trails off as I turn around, grabbing her and pulling her towards the hallway, nodding my regret towards Pearl as I go. Stopping only to unlock the door of my room, my hold of her never ceases as we walk into my room. Turning around abruptly as we enter the room, I push her up against the door before my mouth reaches hers. We start a heated kiss struggling for control, which I have no intention of losing. Waiting her out takes a few minutes, but in that time she stops fighting and gives into me. As soon as I feel her relax against me, I reward her with my hands traveling across her body.

Stopping as my hands reach her large breasts, I tug the tight shirt she is wearing up and over those luscious tits, before dragging the cup of her bra down. Pinching on her nipple, the sounds coming from her let me know that she is enjoying this little game, but I know that she needs more, and I have talked with Bull about the pain that she says she needs. I will give it to her because she is the only thing that I can think of and the only woman that I have ever wanted to claim. SHE. IS. MINE.

Reaching down to her ass, I pull her thighs up as she wraps her legs around me and I continue the kiss. Moving towards the bed, I drop her to her feet and simply say, "Strip." Turning around I move towards my closet and throw over my shoulder, "and bend over the end of my bed, Spitfire. NOW!" Turning towards the closet, I notice the door open slightly and know that Bull is not able to resist the draw to this woman either. Seeing him enter, and quickly shut and lock the door behind himself, I smile knowing this woman is in for something tonight.

Opening the closet, I grab the paddle that I had made for our Spitfire out and examine the burnt wood. Looping it around my wrist I grab up the cane that I also purchased and turn back towards the woman that has haunted my dreams since the night we met. "You want the pain,

Spitfire?" I say cutting the distance separating us, I look at the beautiful sight of her bent over the end of my bed: beautiful in just her nakedness and submission. Her head nods as she holds the position she got into. "The words, Spitfire, you know I will need the words, if we give this to you. And know, that there will be no other man allowed near you again, Spitfire. NONE. EVER."

Running a hand over her round ass, I see that the marks she got from Theo are faded. I know that she is probably in need of something by this point. Pinching a cheek, I bend over to kiss the hurt away before swatting her. "Answer me, Spitfire. Is this what you want?"

"Yes," comes out of her lips, breathlessly.

"You will belong to us, Spitfire. No more Theo, no more finding another man to take care of your wants, your desires, your needs. Only we will be the ones you kneel for and submit to. Only we will be the ones you bend over a bed for. Just us that you will listen and take commands from. Only to us will you present that hot cunt, tight little asshole, and luscious fucking mouth to. ONLY US."

Looking from Bull towards me, she pauses only momentarily, "Yes," pausing for long seconds I wait to see how she will address me before we move on. "Country. Bull."

Swatting her ass with my hand, I growl, "Not Country. Not Bull. Try again Spitfire."

"Sir's?" She squeaks out questioningly, and I groan at the thought. Landing another slap to her ass, I think that in this moment my girl may not know as much about us as I would like her to. She will never guess the name that I would like for her to call me, after all we really do not know each other that well, yet.

"Master Wayne and Master Johnathan" she stutters out slowly and I find myself stepping back from her. Looking at Bull, I see the longing in him, and wonder if Heather is ready for this. Bending over, I nip at her ear before whispering. "That is exactly what we would like for you to call us, Spitfire. Please tell me if this is not okay with you. We will give you this chance to tell us if this is not something you think you can handle. I want you, and you know that. Bull wants you just as much and if you are okay with it we would love to have you between us, for the foreseeable future."

Her eyes go wide as she realizes what I am saying. Her eyes dart between mine and Bull's and I see her mind churning as it works over her answer. Looking towards Bull, I wonder if his thoughts are racing as quickly as mine in the moments it is taking for her to answer.

 It feels like it has been hours before she looks up between Bull and me saying the words that we have both longed to hear from her.

"Masters, I would like nothing more than to give both of you my body. Use me as you both see fit."

Her knowing the name that only she has or will ever call me makes my cock hard. Rewarding her with the pain that she longs for seems like the ultimate praise for her. I step back into her and caress the ass that is now reddening up from the slaps I have landed. I swing the paddle around and catch the wooden handle in my hand before leaning forward over her. Placing the paddle next to her face on the bed, I growl into her ear, "Look at the paddle that I've had made for you, my Spitfire. After you get your fill of looking, make sure to give it a kiss before it gives you that pain you are looking for."

Seeing her head rise slowly and turning on its side, I see the moment that she realizes what this paddle truly means, and the smile that crosses her face brings me a joy that I have never felt. Seeing the flames burnt into the wood and the word Spitfire that is carved out in the middle of the paddle, her eyes roam it freely for long minutes, before she leans towards it, and not only kisses, but loves every inch of it with her tongue, before pulling back saying, "Thank you both, so much for letting that gorgeous paddle mark my skin, Master Wayne. I have never been as happy as I am right now. Thank you," trails off as she buries her head back into the bed.

Heather does not make so much as a whimper from the first blow of the paddle, letting me know that the pressure I have put behind it, is not enough for her. Giving her pain, is something that has taken me the majority of two weeks to come to a decision about. Grams helped point me in the right direction when I was over there a few days ago. Telling me straight out that I was "a dumb ass, if I didn't give whatever it was that the woman who had me looking so sad, wanted." Then smacked me on the back of the head before pushing me back outta the door.

Bull on the other hand, was much quicker to accept what Heather feels she needs. Stepping closer, he extends his hand, silently asking for the paddle, which I have no issue giving up to him. As I move towards the head of the bed I see Heather smile before Bull's first strike lands. The smile quickly fades away with each strike he lands. Continuing to amp up the force he puts behind the paddle, quickly her ass is raised and welted resembling the patterns that have been burned into her paddle. Soon the groans that are coming from her lips are joined with tears streaming down her face.

Against my desires, we spoke with Theo about Heather, the day after his last session with her. I let him know first and foremost that she was ours, and that his services were no longer required anywhere near her. After we worked through that we actually had quite a nice little chat about our Spitfire, the pain slut. Theo let me know that he has never had a woman who could tolerate as much as she can.

"I have used the crop, whip, and cane on her in the same night, and only started to reach the outskirts of her boundaries. I find myself tiring out long before she has met her limits, that is for damn sure." Theo says thinking back on our little Spitfire.

Slugging his shoulders to draw him outta his memories, I wonder aloud, "I wonder if the pain will be better mixed in with sex?"

"She doesn't have sex, Country. Not with any of the Dommes or Doms- even when she was going to clubs in

New Orleans, she didn't as far as she told me. She says that sex is too personal, that the pain is all she needs from any of us. That her sexual appetites do not go hand in hand with the relief she feels from pain."

Looking towards him, Bull asks, "Do you think that is possible? She comes to a fucking BDSM club for the pain she seeks and that's all?"

"Yes, but I have seen some other scars on her that I think might not have come by those same means. The pain she gets at the club is something that she considers acceptable, instead of other methods of pain."

Nodding my head, I ask him about any other Doms or Dommes that she might have sessioned with, and he points out a few. While talking with them, they have all told us the same. She has an extreme tolerance for pain, and none of them have ever touched her in a sexual manner. She has offered to let them use her mouth, if they so need, but each and every time the men and women seemed only too excited to try and break the pain slut. None of them have ever succeeded though.

Bringing my thoughts back to the present, I grab for the whip as Bull lowers the paddle onto her ass with more force and is rewarded with another small murmur from her lips. Running his fingertips over her heated ass, she draws a sharp breath as I bend over, licking the tears away from her face.

"Spitfire, however does your ass feel." Raising up I lean over to get a better glimpse of Bull's handiwork. "It looks so pretty all marked up by the gorgeous paddle." Landing a sharp slap to it, I ask again, "Tell me how it feels."

"Master Wayne, it feels delicious." Turning her head to rest her cheek on the bed she smiles, "Master Johnathan has done a wonderful job with the paddle. I want more."

"You do, do you? Well, let me see what I can do about that."

Pulling the whip free from my shoulder, I move to stand behind Heather. Bull moves to the head of the bed and slowly strokes a hand down Heathers cheek. Moving in slowly I see their hesitation, before they finally connect, and the kiss is heated and passionate, and has me wanting to sink into her. Moving to the side, I land another few licks with the whip before, adjusting again and moving back to the left side of the foot of the bed.

"You look so pretty marked up for us, Spitfire. Just a few more and the fun will really begin." Landing a few more to each side, I quickly drop the whip before moving swiftly over to the closet, grabbing out a rather large vibe and butt plug tossing them onto the bed next to Heather, I notice her eyes go wide as she takes them in. Grabbing the lube that Bull has dug outta the dresser next to the bed I move towards her applying a generous amount onto the plug before teasing her tight asshole with more. Moving the plug to the puckered ringlet, I start my slow intrusion with it. The moans and groans spilling from her lips only drive me on.

"When we spoke with Theo, he let us know that you only took the pain when you were sessioning with any Dommes or Doms, I would like to see if having you cumming helps with your pain tolerance at all. Would you like that, my Little Spitfire?"

"Whatever you would like to do or give me is-" Cutting her off quickly I yank at her hair bringing her face to meet mine before saying these next words.

"Don't you dare be one of those mindless subs, Heather, you are more than that. You tell us what you are thinking, not what you think that we want to hear or what you think that you are supposed to say. The only way this thing will work is if we are all honest with each other. You are in no way a submissive that could give in to living the lifestyle fully, you are here for the pain and we all know it. Just answer my questions honestly, Heather, that is all we are asking."

"Ok Wayne, I-" before she can go on, I attack her mouth with my own. Hearing her use my given name so freely has me wanting to bury myself inside of her and never come out. Releasing her from my grasp I step back and again ask, "Would you like to try mixing pain and pleasure?"

"Yes, I think that I would like to try that with you, Master Wayne."

 And with that I resume my ministrations to her lush body, as Bull resumes consuming her mouth with his own.

CHAPTER ELEVEN

HEATHER

Popping the plug into my ass has it on fire. I'm not sure if Wayne doesn't realize that I haven't had much sex in the past six years or what, but he is not taking it easy on me. The burn radiating through my body from my ass only intensifies the feeling of him as he trails his hands over the welts that are coming to the fleshy globes of my ass. I hear him behind me and know that he has dropped his pants. As I feel him behind me, I feel his rock hard cock rubbing through my folds and know that the burning in my ass is only about to get more intense. As he nudges himself into me, I feel myself gasp at the burn and fullness of having both the plug and his cock buried deep. When I am almost too consumed in thoughts of the fire running through me, Johnathan leans in and starts kissing me again. When I am lost to his mouth, he reaches over and starts pinching my nipples while the assault comes to a climax fighting from both Wayne and myself.

The next few weeks pass by with much of the same. Spending the days at work, getting the most out of the precious time that Sophie is home from school before she goes to bed, and getting plans together for the surprise wedding that Doc talked me into helping out with. I was assigned to work on the scene at The Dungeon and I feel more at home there then I would've been if I got stuck with Sara's duty of the clubhouse. I think we have a good plan for the wedding and I have set up a good scene for Ember and her partner to enjoy, I'm not sure if Doc is going to be the one playing or if he will let Pearl be the one, but either way I have my bases covered.

Taking Sophie over to Irene's house around bedtime almost every night, I find myself heading to the clubhouse or The Dungeon to spend time with Wayne and Johnathan. They have mastered my body and its need for pain, surprisingly well, each in their own way.

As we are laying together naked in Bull's room at the clubhouse two nights before the wedding, they bring up wanting to meet Sophie. Saying that they would like for it to happen before the big event since all of the kids will be around then. I am taken back by their question and desire, I don't have any idea why, either. They have not led me to believe that this was just a passing thing, for fucks sake they have all but claimed me in front of their brothers and I am sure that my mouth is still wide open from the thought, when they look toward me I lose almost all self-control.

"Spitfire, why is it taking you so long to answer us? We are together, you are ours, and that little girl will be a big part of our family when we get our ring on your finger and our ink on your skin. I'm not sure what you are finding an issue with right now, but just be warned there is a right and wrong answer here, Spitfire."

Pulling away slowly, I turn to look first at Johnathan's then Wayne's pained eyes and know that I fucked this up again. "Sorry, Wayne, Johnathan, I guess I never thought about it. I should have and it has never crossed my mind that you might want to meet Soph. She is such a noisy little thing, and she knows about both of you, of course, but it just never crossed my mind to have you come over. She has seen some of the texts that you both have sent and the flowers you have had delivered as well." Dropping my eyes down, I take a deep breath before steadying myself and locking eyes with Wayne again. "Is that something that you would like Wayne? Johnathan?" Seeing the smile take over their faces, they only nod, before my lips claim first Wayne's then Johnathan's lips in a heated kiss.

I decide tomorrow is as good a day as any, and Wayne and Johnathan both agree. As we dress, we start to make plans for tomorrow. Knowing that Sara and Gun are still at each other's throats, I wonder if doing it at our house is the right thing. Seeing the warring going on within me, Wayne steps into me quickly. "My house will be fine Heather. Grams would love to finally meet you and then you don't have to get the anxiety that I am sure is coursing through you with your concerns for Sara." Looking towards Bull, I nod my head as he agrees with me.

Smiling, I look towards them, "You know my thoughts too well. It's kinda freaky how you knew what I was thinking just then. Well, really most of the time you know it."

"Come on, let's get you back to your house, so you can get Sophie settled in her bed. We will expect you over early tomorrow though, Spitfire. We will spend the day together, I can make us a picnic lunch and we can walk over to the park and enjoy the afternoon together."

Both helping me up and off of the bed, I try to get my clothing back on, but find my body very sore and my movements are slow. Bending over, I grab up my dress and raise my arms up slowly before slipping it over my head. The skirt of the dress catches on my hips and I need to shimmy it down with my hands so that it falls back in place. Glancing back towards both Johnathan and Wayne, who have neither made a move since helping me outta the bed, to get their clothing on. I find them both rock hard. They have not sorted any of their clothing out, they are both just standing there next to the foot of the bed, staring at me. Looking them both over, I groan as I take note of their rock hard cocks, which they are lazily stroking back and forth, while licking their lips as each of their eyes take turns boring into mine.

Continuing their eye fucking, Country's voice grows husky as he speaks, "Back on the bed, Spitfire, Hands and knees, hike that dress back up to your hips, where it seemed to have such a problem before. I need to fuck my tight little cunt one last time before we go." Slowly stroking over his dick again, he looks up at me before adding, "That was certainly some little show that you were putting on for us. If you wanted to have more of my cock or his tonight, Spitfire all you had to do was ask. Now your ass is about to pay for it."

Doing as he has asked, I pull my skirt up over my hips before moving sluggishly towards the bed. Most of my joints are aching, but I don't want to disappoint him or

Johnathan, so I do as he says. Crawling to the middle of the bed I arch my back and settle myself into a comfortable position, before I feel the bed sag next to me, I find myself taking a deep breath. Feeling his fingertips travel over and up my legs, he reaches my pussy, a sigh leaves my lips at his gentleness.

As the bed sags, I feel warm breath on my ear before Johnathan speaks. "You are always so wet for us, my Little Spitfire. But, I think that we may need to hold off tonight, Wayne. Heather, answer me honestly in this," he says skimming his hand over my ass. "That wasn't a seductive show you were putting on for our eyes only, was it? You are sore, we have worked you over too hard these past weeks, right?"

Nodding my head, I answer instantly, "Yes, Master Johnathan that is exactly right. My body is very sore and that is why I was moving the way I was when you were both watching me so intently. I wasn't trying to put on a show or be a brat."

Stroking along my ass again, he slowly tugs my skirt down and helps me to my feet again. "Lay on your belly then for a bit and let me rub some of that tension outta your muscles before we go."

"Johnathan, honestly if I lay down, I will fall asleep." Smiling towards him, I slowly place my hand on his chest as I lean into him, kissing him first on the cheek and then on the mouth. Our tongues swirl together for long moments before I feel Wayne come up behind me, running his hands over my hips pulling me into him slightly. Feeling their cocks throb against my skin has me wishing I wasn't as sore as I am. Wishing that their cocks were buried deep inside of me instead of them showing me their care for me by putting their needs on hold.

"Let's get you home then, maybe your body will be singing a different tune. Either way, when you come over tomorrow, bring your swim suit and Sophie's so we can take a soak in the hot tub" Squishing me in between them, my mind again goes to the hard cocks against my flesh.

"Masters, would you like me to take care of that for you," I say with a smile on my lips.

"No Spitfire, we will be fine. You have given us both blue balls enough these last few months, I am sure one more case of it will not be the death of either one of us."

Moving slowly from the bed, they get dressed and are ushering me outta the clubhouse before I realize it. Putting me into the passenger seat of my truck, Bull goes around to the driver's door. As he gets in, I have the keys out for him before he can ask. Country's bike comes alive next to us, and we are off. Making our way home, I notice he doesn't ask for or need directions as to the way to my home. I wonder if it is because of Sara, Irene, or me that this is the case.

Again, like he is reading my mind, he answers the unasked question. "We have both come over to Irene's house with Gun a few times, when he would make his weekly trips over there." Smiling wide in the dim he reaches up to his lips as he speaks, "Not that either one of us hasn't been over a few times since we started this thing between us, to check up on you because I know for sure that we both have."

Chuckling at their stalker tendencies, I reach over and grab his hand away from his lap and intertwine our fingers together. "I have never done the same thing with the clubhouse or Country's place over on Spring Street."

Squeezing my hand tightly, he laughs deeply as the realization sets in for him. "So I don't need to give you directions over to his house then, huh?"

CHAPTER
TWELVE

COUNTRY

I should not have let things get outta hand with her body the way I have these last few weeks. Bull and I have just not been able to stop ourselves whenever we are around her. I knew that once I had her, and we claimed her as our own, I wouldn't be able to temper this raging hard on for her. When she admitted how sore she was to us, I knew the mistake we made and knew what we needed to do. We would help her into her house, and make sure she was comfortable, maybe give her a massage and then leave her till the morning.

We made sure to go into the house with her, even going so far as heading next door with her to pick up Sophie off the couch and carry her into her bed. Pulling up outside of the house, I didn't miss Preach's bike parked along the street. What I wasn't expecting was walking in on him and Irene making out over the kitchen table. Looking towards Heather and Bull, we clear our throats in unison before Preach pulls away from Irene. Glancing towards me then Bull, he only nods before walking down the hall. Irene's cheeks flush a bright red, as she holds her robe closed tighter and kisses Heather on the cheek before scurrying from the room as well. Shaking my head as I look at Heather, she has a hard time stifling the laugh that is trying to break free from her lips. Putting my finger to her lips, I motion towards a sleeping Sophie on the couch and see her recognition instantly. Bull has already made his way towards the couch and is picking up the girl, before we make our way over there. We head back out the door without another shared moment between us.

Watching Heather just in these few minutes since we've come home, I feel even worse about how we have been using her body. She has a fucking kid and she needs to be able to get shit done around the house let alone when she has to work. The sooner that we make her ours the easier it will be to help with those kind of things. I will take it to the brothers soon, I know it seems quick but I can't see my life without her in it and I know that Bull feels the same way. She shouldn't be doing all this shit on her own, and it makes me want to try and talk to her again about her ass of an ex. The first time we tried to talk about him, she only skirted the topic and ended up getting quite the whipping for it. She was blatantly dishonest in our discussions about him and the things that she would reveal to me had little or no real substance to them. I wish she would have trusted us more, but it had been in the early going of this thing between us.

After she has tucked Sophie in bed, she backs quietly outta the room, and turns to us. "Thanks for the help with Sophie, Wayne and Johnathan" Placing a hand on my chest she leans into me and rests her head on my shoulder. Without thought, I scoop her up into my arms, and stride towards her room with Bull quickly on my heels. Placing her gently on her bed, I remove her shoes slowly, kissing her feet, ankles, and up to her knees before pulling back. Her mouth is dropped open as I lean back down to worship this woman that has given herself to us. Pushing her skirt up as I make my way towards her pussy, I catch the smell of pears, mixed with her musky scent.

Looking up I see Bull working over her shoulders, breasts, and arms with his hands and mouth as I continue my assault on her pussy. The moans and groans are filled with pleasure both from the massage and the way I am eating her pussy. Tugging her down the bed gently, the skirt travels up her body as I move her towards the edge. I continue the kisses that I have been placing all over her lower body. She wiggles outta Bull's hold and makes quick work of removing the dress and I see it fly to the laundry basket before she settles down on the bed again. Looking up at her beautiful breasts, my cock throbs in my pants with want.

"Turn over Heather, we wanna rub your sore muscles before we leave tonight." As she tries to protest Bull hushes her quickly, "If you fall asleep here, it won't matter. And you want to do as we ask, don't you Little Spitfire?"

"Yes, I do." Is all I hear before her body is rolling over, and she is resting with her belly against the bed. Her head is turned to the side, as her eyes fight to stay open. "Sleep if you will darlin, I will be here early to pick you and Sophie up and bring you over to my house to meet Grams. Bull will come over when he gets done with some errands for the club, then we can have that picnic and spend the afternoon together." Feeling her relax as I start the massage on her legs and Bull starts on her shoulders and back, I make note to never neglect this beautiful fucking body again. As I roam my hands over her lower back and ass, I see our marks from last week with the cane and a smile comes to my face remembering that night.

When I ran into her last week at The Dungeon, I noticed the marks on her before I even pulled her into my arms for a kiss. The marks that she better hope to fuck, she has a good explanation for, because if I so much as sense that she has been near another, I will fucking lose it. And her ass will definitely be worse for it.

Getting Bull's attention away from the scene he is watching, I let him know that we are heading into a room with our Spitfire. Pulling her towards a free room, I see the door close behind us as Bull enters. I move her arms up to the light, seeing the small bruises that trail up and down both of her arms, my heart lurches. "What are these, Spitfire?" Looking into her eyes, I see the moment when realization strikes her and guilt consumes her. Bull is next to me in that second, running his fingers up and down her arms.

"We told you, that we were the only ones to give you pain or pleasure, Heather." Joining my fingers with Bull's we continue to run them over her arms, I can't help but wonder if these are the only new marks on her pale flesh. "This looks to me like you were taking what was not yours to take, is that not the case, Spitfire?"

"Wayne- "

Bull cuts her off quickly, "NO, Little Spitfire. Master when we are in here and you are facing punishment for doing something that we directly told you not to do. You better fucking tell us right now where these have come from, and heaven help you if you came to anyone here giving something that is no longer yours to give, instead of coming to one of us." Pulling the shirt from her body, I make a fast pass over her chest looking for more evidence of damage.

Those big brown eyes meet mine, and I see the pain in them as she whispers, "I would never do that, Master Johnathan. You are the ones that own me, I just needed something to calm my nerves after something happened this week." Not knowing what could have happened I pull away looking again at the marks on her body and up towards Bull.

When I see his eyes, I know that there are more marks. He looks down and my gaze follows his, when I look down to see what he has seen, I notice that she has made small cuts from something in and around her stomach. I am guessing she put them there to better hide them, and even trying to keep it from us. Bending down, I kiss each mark on her stomach as Bull does the same to her arms, drawing small gasps from her, "This was not your pain to give, Spitfire. These should have been mine to give to you or Master Johnathan's. You really need to learn to ask for the things that you need. We are the ones that you belong to. You agreed and it is not something that we will let fall to the side or go without punishment. We will talk more as to why you felt the need to give yourself these," pointing to the bruises on her arms, then to the marks on her stomach, "and these, but first we need to mark you by our own hands. Strip and lean over the bed, this is going to hurt."

"Yes, Masters." Is out of her lips as she shrugs outta her clothing before placing herself over the edge of the bed. Sticking her lush ass up high in the air causing my dick to stir. Looking at Bull, he nods before heading to the cupboard grabbing a few things out. He grabs out a thick cane and gives it a go against his palm. Handing it to me, I do the same and feel the sting with the first strike. I know that this will give her the pain she needs, and the marks that we need as well. Striding towards her, I don't hesitate before bringing the cane down on her ass, drawing a gasp from her lips. The cries that come from her mouth as I continue the assault on her ass and thighs are only quieted by the momentary gasps for breath, which are quickly muted as Bull rams his cock in her mouth. As I look down towards her the tears that are streaming down her face, ruining her mascara and eye makeup and the cock that Bull is driving into her mouth, only makes my cock harder.

She is so beautifully dirty and ready to fly for us. That is not something she will get tonight though and we all know it. She needs to learn that she has to come to me or to Bull for everything or this shit between us will never work. We both told her when this shit started that if we were going to do this, we were going to do it all. I have given her the pain as best I can, Bull has done wonders with the pain he is able to deal out as well. He has a heavy hand when it comes to our Spitfire, but that is something that she definitely needs.

If she doesn't tell us, be honest with herself and with us at all times, we can't possibly fill her needs and desires.

Whack "Spitfire, you will come to us with everything." Whack. "You will come to us when you have needs." Whack. "You will come to us when you have desires." Whack. "You will come to us when you think you shouldn't." Whack. "You will always come to us, Spitfire." Whack. "No matter what your mind or body might be telling you." Whack

Seeing the welts forming on her luscious and curvy ass I know that I have been rough and that these marks will be there for weeks to come. "Don't reinjure these Heather. If you need pain or a reminder of our lessons, please, you only have to ask one of us."

Only after Johnathan has pulled his cock free from her mouth does she answer. "Yes, Master Wayne, Master Johnathan. I understand and am sorry that I didn't come to either one of you. I know that I should have, but I was just too weak."

Stroking along her shoulder I hush her, before letting her know, "You will always come to me or John, or the punishment will be ten times worse than what we just gave you." Seeing her leaking down her leg, has me letting my cock free from my pants. As I line my dick up with her pussy, I let her know, "No cumming for you Spitfire. This is to remind you that you belong to us. Don't pull this shit again or we will not be so forgiving." Sinking into her, I know that this is only the beginning of her rebellion, she hates being told what to do, unless she is submitting to us fully, and when she does she loves serving us, that is when she can free herself enough to let go.

When I shake myself out of the thoughts of that night, I find Heather sleeping. Getting off of her slowly, I pull up the quilt on her bed, tucking her in tight before bending to kiss her forehead. I notice that Bull is double checking the doors and windows before he heads back into the room to kiss Heather. Checking on Sophie and even Sara before heading outta the house helps me feel safer about leaving them here, even though I know that Bull will be staying outside for the night. We are struggling not to startle or frighten her away, but we have to ask what happened to bring on her incident last week injuring herself. We have wanted to ask her but just haven't. We have also talked about getting her to move in for weeks. We know that we have never met Sophie before but if she is half of the person her mother is we know that we will love her in an instant. Bull and I have decided to stay at my house, until Grams can no longer be on her own. Being near her puts my mind at ease, and having Heather and Sophie under our roof with us will put our minds at somewhat of ease.

As we lock up the house behind us, we notice a BMW parked across the street from our bikes. It's a nice fucking car, but seems sorta outta place here in this neighborhood. As we walk towards our bikes, a prospect brought Bull's over, I take note of the license plate and make sure to dial in a favor with Tank about finding out who the fuck it is. Nodding at Bull, we pull out together, but I know that he is just going around the block and I am more than happy that he will be here watching over our girls.

The next morning comes quickly, and I find myself with a bag full of donuts and coffees at her door before eight. Bull is off his bike as I make my way towards the door, and lets me know that the BMW pulled away when he came back around after circling the block. I let him know that I have called in a favor with Tank and he will let us know when he finds anything out. Knocking on the door, Sara answers it in a t-shirt and pair of boxers looking mean as a bear caught in a trap. Rolling her eyes as she sees that it is us, which is only short lived when she notices the box of Firecake Doughnuts and coffee that I got in my hand.

The smile that spreads across her face, is matched only with the shriek I hear coming from the staircase. Sophie and Heather are both headed at us full speed. Neither stopping to talk to either Bull or myself, only pausing briefly to grab the box of donuts outta my hand and head towards the kitchen. I guess that was a good idea, and I will definitely be stopping at that little shop more frequently.

As Sophie looks me over, she quickly finishes her doughnut before getting up outta her chair and walking up to me. Tugging at my shirt sleeve, I get up outta my chair before kneeling down to her. I smile wide as she introduces herself to me.

"Hey. I'm Sophie. You are my mommy's friend right? Wayne? She talks about you a lot and sometimes I even need to tell her to be quiet, she goes on and on about you." With a giggle she reaches up touching the Stetson I still have fixed on my head. Looking towards my feet she also takes note of the cowboy boots I have donned. "Are you a cowboy or something? Do you have a horse?"

"No, Princess I am not. But, I could probably become one for you."

"No, I don't think I want a cowboy. I like that guy Gun that comes over to Irene's house sometimes to talk with her. He is always nice and he doesn't scare me. That guy, Preach seems nice too, but sometimes him and Irene kiss and it is so gross. Are you like either of those guys?"

Quirking an eyebrow up at her slip, I ask with a smile on my face. "You want me to be old Princess?"

"NO, not old like them. They are just super nice, and I see Preach hugging Irene and holding hands with her when they think I'm not looking. He seems to like her, and even Gun likes Auntie Sara but they fight a lot. So don't do that, not with my mom. She has been so nice, and such a good mom to me, I think that you make her happy and I just want to make it easy for you to make her happy."

"Princess, you never have to worry about that. I will do everything in my power to make your momma and you as happy as I can, Ok?"

"Ok Wayne, that's good." Walking the few steps over to Bull, I watch her pull on his shirt like she did to mine. "Then you're Johnathan, right? You are the other guy my mom talks about." Moving down to one knee in front of her, Bull nods his head in response.

"Yes, Princess, I am."

"You are big," she says with wide eyes looking over Bull's wide frame. I am a big guy and Bull has probably six inches and fifty pounds on me. Looking around from Bull to me, when her eyes land on her mommy she asks, "So, mommy am I going to have two dads like Iris, Rose, and Rebel have? That would be so cool, going from having no dads to having two."

Looking up at me and then towards Bull, the shock that takes over her face, leaves me with no question that she is still doubting this thing between us. Before I speak, Bull has scooped up Sophie and has her on the counter leaning over her as he speaks words that have never been truer. "We want nothing more than that Sophie. But, your momma and us still need to work out the details before that can happen." Looking around at me and then Heather, as his eyes reach hers again he simply asks, "Is that something that you would like Princess?"

"Yup, that's what I want." Looking around and back to him, Sophie asks, "Can we go to the park for that picnic now?"

"Of course, we can. First let's head over to my house and get a real breakfast in you two." He says helping her off the counter as she runs for her ma.

Looking from Sophie I glance up towards Heather before saying in her direction, "Well we can go if your ma is ready to get a move on, that is."

Hearing Bull from across the room, I laugh at the balls on him, "If her ma is ready? Ha! You might as well get a move on either way."

Cutting the distance between myself and Sophie, I grab her up off the floor and move the few inches towards her mom when her giggles overtake my senses. Placing her up onto the cupboard next to her Ma, I ruffle her hair as her giggles stifle out. I look towards Heather before closing the distance to her and wrapping my arms around her waist as I lean in and kiss her hard. As Bull moves in behind her and steps into her back running his hands over her hips.

CHAPTER
THIRTEEN

HEATHER

After Wayne picked us up, with a car seat already installed in his old Chevy truck. We drive the short distance over to his house, where he has already made breakfast, warming it up as we enter the kitchen. The donuts and coffee that he brought over were only an appetizer it seems. The first thing I notice is the clean rustic feel of his house. Sophie runs from room to room playing with the coon hound, Rascal, that Wayne is only too happy to have playing with someone who has so much energy.

As I help set the table with napkins and silverware, Wayne plates up the food and points out the cupboard with the glasses and mugs. I grab a couple of each out and place them on the table. Heading to the fridge, I open the door and look for the juice, before I feel his arms wrap around me and his lips on my neck.

"Those pears you smell of haunt my fucking dreams darlin'. Come wash up for breakfast and I'll finish up down here." Pulling away from him, he gently prods me up the stairs towards the second floor of his house. As I go, I hear him say, "Sophie, would you like apple or orange juice, Princess?"

Heading into the bathroom, I wash up and notice that the same soaps and lotions that I use at my house are here on the sink. Thinking that might be too close a similarity, I head to the shower and see my pear scented wash, shampoo, and conditioner all in the shower as well. Feeling slightly freaked out, I take a few deep breaths before making my way outta the bathroom. I find myself not being able to stop myself from looking into the doors as I pass. When I reach the last door I pull it open and am stunned at what I see inside. Stepping inside I am drawn in by the view that finds me, this must have been two rooms at some point, which are in the midst of becoming one large suite. It must be his bedroom, the master of this house, it has a humungous four poster bed situated near various BDSM equipment and furniture in different stages of assembly. I stand for long moments, before I am able to start my feet moving and head towards the men that will need to explain this shit, right fucking now.

Slamming the door before moving back down the hallway I walk back into the kitchen, I see that Sophie is still not sitting at the table, and know I gotta talk to them before this freaks me out even worse. "Wayne we need to talk. Now."

Wayne looks up at me from the counter, turning around slowly as I step into the room. His eyes go wide as he takes in my anger. Wayne is the first to speak, "Spitfire, what do you have that look for, you went upstairs to wash up, what could have happened?"

"Why is there all those soaps and shit that I use, that my daughter uses in your bathroom, Wayne? That shit is just fucking weird. I just walked into your house for the first time, and it feels so much like I have already been here, like it is somewhere that I can see myself fitting into well."

"You need to calm down, Spitfire. We are here enjoying the day with Sophie and Bull when he gets here, and if you work yourself up I will not hesitate to drop Sophie off with Grams or Irene or even one of the brothers and take it out on you."

"Wayne you have to admit-"

"Stop! Spitfire. If you are going to act like this, then you will call me Master. But, that is not how this is going to go down, so just stop. I have bought those things and supplied them here, just like in my room at the clubhouse, and my locker at The Dungeon, just as Bull has done. You are usually flying too high to even notice when we are doing aftercare on you, I'm guessing, to have seen them before. We are your lovers, your masters, and will soon take it to the brothers to make you our ol' lady as well as our wife, so we will take care of you in all ways and all things."

"What about that master bedroom? What do you have to say about all of the stuff in there? It looks like you have been working on that for a while and we have only been together for a few weeks."

"Spitfire, whatever were you doing up there, digging around our room? I only asked you to head upstairs to wash up for breakfast, but you felt like snooping instead?"

"Our room, what are you talking about Wayne?"

"We have been working on that room for a while, Heather. I was hoping, no, we were hoping," walking towards me, I notice him reach into his pants pocket before he answers. "That could be our room. That you and Sophie would move in here with me and Bull, and that we could all help to make this house a home. I know that this is moving fast, and that we haven't known each other even half a year, but this thing, us being together needs to happen." Pulling the key outta his pocket a smile crosses his lips as he sees my face drop thinking that it was a ring.

Relaxing as I realize that his words are true and that they have had those things for me, but this is only the first time that I have noticed, stabs me in the heart knowing the conclusions I had drawn. Stepping forward, I glance behind me and see that Sophie and the dog are headed upstairs to play as I drop to my knees in front of him. "I'm sorry, Master."

Standing he pets my head slowly stroking through my hair, before bending over to grab under my arms and pull me to my feet. "Spitfire, never take to your knees calling me Master while our girl is here running about, please. We can play at The Dungeon or the clubhouse, but, never with her so close." Wrapping his arms around me, I feel safe there covered up in him. "Your happiness has been our first priority for months, now that you have blessed us with Sophie's trust, she has found her place next to you in our hearts. Spitfire, you never answered my question though. Will you move in with us?"

Letting him know, that I would like nothing more than to move in, we call for Sophie as we settle in and have a delicious breakfast before heading next door. I am surprised to not only meet Grams, but Wayne's mother is there as well. They are both so kind and down to Earth and I know exactly where Wayne's warmth and love comes from. As we spend the majority of the later morning and early afternoon together I learn a lot of Wayne's past and glimpses into the child that he once was. I hear stories of his childhood antics and when Grams has taken Sophie outside to play in the yard, I hear the stories that no mother should have to relive about how her son saved her from his father. She isn't shy about telling them, and I think it's to give me some of the prologue to the story of him, my Country. Spending this time with them, makes me long for the extended family that Sophie and I have never had. As we leave to head to the park we make plans for dinner the next week and I hope that this is something that will be happening more.

As we start towards the park, Wayne skedaddles home to grab the picnic basket before catching up with us down the block. Watching him with Soph has me so happy that I was lucky enough to find this man and only long for the time that we can be doing these things with Johnathan as well. The men look at me like I am the dawn and the dusk of their days. Wayne looks at my daughter much the same way, and I am guessing it will be the same with Johnathan. I know that when we become a family it will be one of the best day of all of our lives.

As we get back to Wayne's house, I notice how tired Soph is and guess that she might actually need a nap. As I kneel down by the chair she sits on I ask, "Soph, hon, you think that maybe you wanna take a nap darlin?" Shaking her head, I go on, "Soph, you were really running around at the park and I don't know what Wayne and Johnathan have planned for tonight, but I don't want you to be tired and crabby or we might have to go home instead of spending the rest of the day with them."

"Momma that isn't fair. You said that we were gonna spend the whole day here. You can't do that. I want to spend the day here, Wayne and Johnathan are fun. Can we get a dog? Wayne's dog is so cool, she loves me, look at her."

"Darlin we can talk about a dog later, stop trying to stall. Back to the matter at hand, your nap."

Shaking her head, Wayne steps next to me and smiles wide as he easily talks my daughter into a nap that she had seemed so against a few seconds ago. "Sophie, honey, you know what? Maybe you could go lay with Rascal, because he always takes a nap at this time, and usually I lay down with him, but I gotta get all the stuff together for tonight, so if you could that would really help me out." Looking between me and Soph he finishes with, "What do you think? Could you help me out? Just this once?"

She nods quickly and he slings her over his shoulder before heading upstairs with Rascal on his heels. About fifteen minutes later he comes back into the living room with a shitty grin on his face.

"What are you so happy about? Did you get her to lay down?" I say looking towards him.

"Yeah, she's sleeping in the spare room with Rascal. I started to set it up a few weeks ago and she must really like it, because she looked around for a few minutes hopped up on the bed, with the dog and was passed out, right quick."

"Must be a honeymoon for you, because there is no way that she would ever have been that easy to get down for a nap for any other reason. I usually fight with her for a good thirty minutes before I give up and let her use her kindle or something."

Stepping into my space, he throws his arms around me before pulling me tight, "Honeymoon, huh? I like the sounds of that! Maybe we could make Sophie a little brother or sister," Reaching out slowly to my stomach, he continues "if we haven't already that is."

"WHAT?"

"Heather, we have been fucking like bunnies for months, and I don't remember you having your period at all during that time. Or are you on birth control?"

"What, well, no, I don't guess that I am" thinking back to the last three months, I think about my lack of a period and my hand shoots to my belly. "Fuck." Moving past Wayne, I grab my keys up off the counter before making my way quickly outta the room, throwing over my shoulder, "I'll be right back."

Making my way to my car, which a prospect dropped off, I hear Wayne calling after me, but my feet won't stop. I need to get to the store and get a pregnancy test. As I reach my car I notice a note under the windshield wiper. Gabbing the note, I almost throw it into the street but I see handwriting that is only too familiar to me. Stopping dead in my tracks I open the paper *I found you again bitch. Don't run this time or I will make it only worse for you and that bitch of a daughter. You stupid cunt, you will not get away from me again. That pain that you are such a fucking freak for- I will help you get that, SOON*

I drop to my knees as the realization sinks in. He's found me. He's coming for Soph and there is no way in hell, he is going to get her. The thoughts of the baby that might or might not be here drops away as I stand quickly rushing back towards the house, still clutching the note in my fucking hand.

Passing by Wayne on the way in the door, he reaches for me but I sidestep around him before he grabs me. "Heather? What's going on? You took outta here like a bat outta hell, and then," reaching for the paper in my hand, he rips it away reading words that will fucking do me in. "This is from him? Zack? You don't have to be scared of him babe, he will not get his hands on you or Sophie. You are ours and we take care of what is ours."

Calming slightly at his words, the thoughts of Zack knowing where I am and where Soph is frightens me to the bone. I nod at Wayne's words but turn slowly wanting to check on her myself. I take the stairs two at a time, before reaching the door where she is still passed out. Rascal, lets out a small growl as I enter the room before he realizes who it is, and settles back into the bed. Seeing that dog's protection of my baby girl sets my mind at ease, somewhat.

Feeling Wayne enter the room a short while later, he is behind me in a second, his smell overtaking my senses instantly. Relaxing back into him, quietly he breaths into my ear, "He will not touch what is ours, Spitfire. Tell me that you understand that? That you know that no man will ever touch you and that any man that tries will be put the fuck down."

As his hands circle around my belly, my thoughts go again to the baby that could be there. SHIT! "Yea I know that you and Johnathan will try to keep me safe. Can you stay with her while I run to the store real quick, Country?"

"You're not going anywhere, Spitfire. I already called Prez and let him know the situation and he is sending a prospect to sit on you until we see what's going on. Bull is on his way to the store to pick up a test or two for us, and then he is heading over to join us for the rest of the day, his errands have ended quicker than he thought." Rubbing his hands up and down my arms, he goes on, "We take care of what is ours and you and that little girl right there," pointing at Soph who is still fast asleep on the bed, "are all ours."

"Prez? Why did you have to call Blaze? Why the hell is there a prospect that has to come over as well. You and Bull will both be here." I say looking away from Wayne embarrassed by the thoughts of Prez knowing about any of this shit.

"That's your issue, with everything that is happening? Prez?" Running a hand through his beard, he goes on holding the note from Zack up to my face. "Prez knowing and the prospects being here, pale in comparison with the other issues that we seem to have going on right now, Heather. Let's focus on your ex, shall we?"

"I don't need to be babysat, Country. I can handle my- "

Holding a finger up to my mouth he cuts me off, "You better watch what you are about to say, Spitfire. Lying to me is not something that will work out well for you, so please don't start." Moving his finger away from my mouth he traces it down my jaw, my chin, my chest, and finally leaves it to rest on my hip. "I know that you are an independent woman, but having an extra set of eyes out there is something that we need, especially with your ex nearby." I try turning from Country but he backs me up the few feet to the wall. Pushing into me with his body. "The prospect is harmless and will be outta sight as far as you and Sophie are concerned. You. Are. Ours. I should not have to remind you of that Spitfire. That first night, months ago I made sure that everyone got that point, Bull and I will take it to the brothers at Church this week." Moving his hand over my belly, "Now, I would like to know if our family is growing."

Hearing a bike pull up we both move together towards the window and see Bull headed to the front door holding a CVS bag. Turning together, we make our way downstairs. Country opens the door before a knock is heard and Bull strides in. Without pause, he hands me the bag and slaps my ass as he walks past saying, "Go get 'em tiger," making

126

his way past me. My eyes don't leave him as he gets to the kitchen pulling open the fridge and grabbing a beer out. Turning around he tosses one to Wayne before popping the top, grinning at me before looking down to the bag still in my hand, "You gonna go find out if we are going to be having a baby with our little wifey or no?"

"Wifey, what are you talking about, Bull?" is all I can manage to get out as confusion falls across my face.

"Well, Country told me that he needed a test, so I just figured it was for you. Was I wrong?" turning towards Country, Bull asks, "Was it not for her? That would be real fucking embarrassing if you got some other chick pregnant at the same time as" hitching a thumb over towards me, "we got our Little Spitfire there pregnant."

With wide eyes Country growls out, "Bull, shut the fuck up. Heather," holding his hand up to me, "we got other shit to deal with right now. We will talk about what he's saying as soon as we get," pointing to the bag in my hand, "that right there sorted out."

CHAPTER FOURTEEN

COUNTRY

Sitting in the master bedroom with Bull and Heather waiting on the test results is the longest three minutes of my life. I hear a bike pull up and glance out the window seeing that the prospect has arrived puts my mind a little more at ease. Bull and I will need to talk about Zack and come up with some sort of plan, which means we will need to get more information from Heather as well. Our usual methods might need to be changed if this test comes out positive, and I decide that calling Tank for not only the license plate info but some advice on Mastering your pregnant sub might be in order.

Hearing the timer ding, all eyes fly to Heather as she walks into the bathroom reaching for the sink. As long seconds pass, she turns slowly around with a smile from ear to ear on her face. Holding up the stick, I see the words before she speaks, "Congratulations daddies." Bull and I are off our seat in short seconds together, before I can scoop her up, Bull has already done it, and I move behind them, engulfing her from behind.

As we let go of our Spitfire, I grab for the box that has also been in my pocket for most of the day. Walking around to the front, next to Johnathan the look we exchange doesn't need words between us. We both drop to our knees and grab for one of our woman's hands. Johnathan is the first to speak.

"We love you so much, Little Spitfire and we have known since the first time that we met you, that first time that our lips connected, not to mention the first time that I saw you taking his cock, or the first time that you took mine, that you were it for me." Squeezing her hand, he slowly brings it towards his lips as I continue on.

"I have loved you just as long, and with every awkward moment that passed between us, I feel for you more. I never thought that you would let me in, let alone both of us and we will make it worth your trust and love each day for the rest of our lives." Dropping her hand, I pop open the box and look to her eyes as she sees the intricate design that Bull and I had made up for the engagement ring. When her eyes meet the matching smaller band, she looks up into my eyes before looking to Bull with the same question on her face. I answer her unasked question, "we had a matching ring made for Sophie as well. Of course her stones are not real," Bull cuts in, "not yet at least," before I go on, "and we will ask her as we have asked you. She is just as big a part of this family and we knew that we would need to make sure that she knows that she is loved just as much as you are."

The tears start falling from her eyes before I am able to get the ring outta the box and onto her finger. Holding the ring box out to her again, she simply nods before Bull helps to take the ring outta the box and slips it onto her finger and at that moment our future begins together.

Celebrating between the three of us and Sophie when she wakes up and also accepts our proposal goes on for much of the rest of the day. We return over to Grams house for dinner, her and Ma are there with wide grins on their faces knowing that our girls are finally coming home. Grams seeing how we used her diamond and set it between the intertwined gold and white gold bands starts crying tears of joy, along with Ma. When we share the news of our growing family, Ma and Grams along with Sophie are each more excited than the last.

Bull and I decide that we will have a few of the brothers come over this week to finish up the master suite as well as Sophie's room so we can get them moved in by next week. The sooner we are under the same roof and able to settle into our daily lives the better.

After I have dropped Sophie, Heather, and Bull off at Heather's I head towards the clubhouse to speak with not only Prez but Tank as well. We want to let them know that we have claimed our woman, and we will soon have yet another Devil's Iron union to set up for.

Running into Prez at the bar first I nod to him, before sitting next to him. "Prez. How are things?"

"Good Country, good. How about with you? How is your Heather doing? Anything from that ex since this afternoon?"

"No, we only saw him that night outside her house, and had that note on her car. She found out that we are pregnant today after we found that note, so we didn't want to stress her out much further. Well, other than putting our ring on her finger and making sure that she couldn't fucking run from us, that is."

Clapping me on the shoulder, Blaze congratulates me, "Let's get some shots together and celebrate for a bit." Looking around Blaze sees Gun, Doc, and Shadow by the pool table, calling them all over to toast with us. Preach is pouring the shots before all the men have even made their way to the bar.

"Brothers, it seems that Country and Bull have gone about their claiming of Heather the same way that the rest of us have, knocking her up before the wedding and ink is put on her flesh. Raise your glasses brothers as we toast to one of the men that will try to keep the little pain slut under wraps."

Cheers are heard from all around as each brother congratulates me in turn.

"I take it, that you and Bull would like to bring that shit to a vote at Church." Nodding my head, he goes on, "Please feel free to ask any and all questions to me or Tank about limits to your little Spitfire while she is pregnant." Pausing briefly an odd smile comes to his lips before he goes on, "Those were some of the best sessions that Tank and I were able to have with Pearl. Challenging as all fucking hell, but rewarding like nothing else. Enjoy it while you can." Clasping me on the back again we enjoy another shot, before I ask about Tanks whereabouts. "He is at home with Pearl tonight, I am guessing you would like whatever he has found out about that plate you wanted him to run, right?" Nodding my head, he goes on, "I will

131

call him and let him know that you are on your way over. Just remember that the wedding is tomorrow and we will not have church until the following day." Looking into my eyes his next words are not taken lightly, "We do this together, brother. No matter what you find out from him, we do this together."

"Yes Prez. I know, I know. Thanks again for the approval, I will see you tomorrow." Turning to Doc I draw him in for a hug, "Enjoy your last night of freedom brother."

I can hear him laughing as I walk away saying, "I will don't you worry. And don't forget, it will be you soon as well, Brother."

It takes me only about a half hour to reach their house, and Tank greets me at the front door. "I hear congratulations are in order, Country." Stepping into the house, I barely make it to his office, before Iris, Rose, and Pearl are surrounding me.

"Country, we heard you and Bull are going to be daddies and that you are getting married!" Rose squawks at me as she wraps herself around one leg as Iris does the same to the other. That is when Pearl engulfs me in a hug as well, happily saying "Congratulations to you guys and Heather. I knew the first time I saw you all together that you would fit together nicely." Taking a few more moments with them, Tank ushers them away before shutting the door behind us.

Moving to his desk, he pulls up the information on the BMW and it is as I suspected. Zack's been watching our girl, and from what Tank can tell, he has been here for about two weeks watching and keeping tabs on her as well as Soph. Not needing any more information in this moment, I thank Tank and head for home, knowing that our celebration and start of our lives will need to be put on hold until this shit with Zack gets sorted out. We will bring claiming her as our ol' lady to the brothers, that shit will not fucking wait.

CHAPTER
FIFTEEN

BULL

After Country dropped Sophie, Heather, and I off, I made sure to do a quick check through the house before we get Sophie situated for bed. I didn't see the BMW outside, but I know that fucker is probably around lurking in some fucking corner waiting to scare our girl even more. Fuck, why couldn't we have just gone over there that night we saw him and taken care of his fucking useless ass then? That would've put her worrying at ease, if nothing else. We don't need our girl stressed out seeing that she is going to have our baby.

OUR BABY! I can still barely believe it even after we made her take all the tests that I brought over to the house. After the fourth one she started really objecting, and I told her that we could keep the other six for the next few babies we have. The look on her face was priceless and the laugh that Country and I exchanged at her expense was something I can only hope we share many more of.

Seeing the way she is with Sophie, I know that we will have to work hard to keep up with how great of a mother she is. At least there will be two of us so maybe we would be able to have a fucking fighting chance.

As Heather gets Sophie ready for bed with a bath, I make sure to reach out to a few of the brothers setting up the work that we will need to get done over the next few days so we can get our home in order before we move our girls in next weekend. We will focus all our energy on Sophie's room and also the master suite and then if there is time the other rooms.

Grams and Country's Ma is so excited at the news of not only our upcoming wedding but the little one that will be joining our family. I think back to my days growing up with five brothers and sisters and know that I would love nothing more than a large family to grow older with. I grab my phone outta my pocket and decide it is past time to call my mom and dad to fill them in on what has been happening these last few months.

Hearing it ring only twice before my mom picks up I wonder where they are at. "Johnathan, my gosh are you alright? We haven't heard from you in so long, your brothers and sisters have said that you have found yourself a girl and that it's pretty serious. That you and Wayne finally found a woman that you could share between the two of you, that will be able to handle you both. Is that why you're calling us? To let us know that you have finally found the one that you are going to bring home to us? Don't make me call Wayne's gram or ma for that matter."

"Jesus Christ Ma, take a breath. Yes, Heather is it for us and yes, I will bring her by as soon as I can to meet the family. Not the only reason I was calling though. She has a daughter named Sophie that you will be happy to learn has decided to call us both daddy, so that means you will be a Grams yourself. Well, and the fact that Heather is pregnant as well."

"Johnathan, oh honey, we are so happy for you. You are finally finding a family up there for yourself, we were all worried that the club might not have been enough." She must pull the phone away from her because her next words are somewhat quieter, "Arthur, Johnathan is on the phone and he has some wonderful news to share." Getting louder, she speaks again, "Honey, your daddy will be right on, please call and let me know when you and Wayne will be down here with your girls, and of course when you will be planning this big day. Here's your daddy now. I love you. Don't be so long in talking with us the next time please."

Taking a breath, I don't know how my dad gets a word in edgewise with her most the time. As I steady myself, my dad gets on the line, "Son, it's good that you finally called, your mom and I were just starting to worry that we haven't heard from you in a while. Been busy up there I hear from what your mom says, huh? Got a little one on the way and a wedding in the works, seems to me that you mighta done that a little backwards, my boy, but as long as it gets done I guess that's what matters."

"Thanks Pops. We will all be moving into Wayne's house by next weekend and I was wondering if you thought maybe Christopher and Joseph would be able to come up and help out during the week?"

"I don't see why not, I will talk to them about it during dinner tonight, and find some coverage on the schedule for them during the week. It's a slow time for us as you can well remember so it shouldn't be a problem."

"Ok, I will get them plane tickets as soon as you give me the go ahead. Thanks for letting them outta work Pops, you know I wouldn't ask if I didn't need their help."

"I know you wouldn't boy. It's not like you call all the time like those sisters of your's having them rush about to hang a fucking picture for them."

Laughing at the thought of Angela and Jessica calling for just that dies in my throat the moment I see Heather walk into the room, with nothing except lust in her eyes. "Pops, my girl just came in, so I'm gonna let you go. Call me after you talk to the twins and please give me at least a day to get the tickets for them to get up here."

"Yeah, yeah son I will. Tell your girl congratulations from us, and that we are looking forward to meeting her and welcoming her into our family."

Disconnecting the call, I toss the phone across the bed, as Heather steps up between my legs, dropping to her knees before I can say a word. The moment her hands reach for my belt, I know that the discussion that I was going to have with her about my family, is going to wait. Because once her hands are on my flesh I am fucking done for.

No words are exchanged between us, as she pulls my cock free. The moment our flesh touches, my dick hardens in her hand, before her mouth is even close to it. Once it is, my dick throbs and pulses its need. As she swallows me down, I cannot stop myself from tangling my fingers into her hair and putting a little pressure on her head. The feeling of her gaging on my cock, only drives me on to wanting more and wanting to go deeper inside of her.

As the tears start to fall from her eyes, I know that I should be worshiping her, instead of treating her as nothing more than my whore, but I can't stop myself. The first time that I feel her swallow around my cock I know that this will not be lasting much longer. The second time she does it I feel my balls start to tingle and tighten. As she swallows one last time, my cock erupts and I growl out, "You take it all, Little Spitfire. You take what I will give you and you swallow it all down, like the good girl that you are. "

As she pops my cock outta her mouth, and looks up at me with those big brown eyes, I am fucking lost for a moment into the feelings I have for her. Scooping her up into my arms, I take her mouth with my own, and can taste myself mixing with her and am instantly hard again. Straddling my hips, I pull her skirt up before moving her panties to the side and sinking deep inside of her.

"Ride me, Spitfire. Make yourself come all over my cock, before I turn your ass over and fuck you on your hands and knees." Putting my hands under her ass, I help to lift her up as she bounces on my cock. After about two minutes, I reach around and stick a finger in her ass before her orgasm takes over her. And I have to bite my cheek to hold off the orgasm that is threatening to push me over."

Cuddling into me, I let her orgasm slowly fade before picking her up and laying her gently on the bed. Kissing her deeply, I make sure to go slowly as I kiss over every inch of our woman's body. I am not sure how we haven't noticed the small changes to her in these last few months but we haven't. I guess we are always too busy trying to bury ourselves inside of her and bring ourselves off to notice the slight changes. The swell of her stomach, the darkening of her nipples, and the sensitivities that are starting to make themselves known as well.

Spending a lot of time on her stomach, I worship our baby and the area that he or she is growing in. Never, would I have thought I would feel such joy at such a thing, but I do. Just like the happiness that I find as her ring glitters in the light and I see the smile on her face as she looks to her hand. Seeing her hand move to her breast, I notice the ring as she is tugging at her nipples, and my cock gets painfully harder. Enough of this, I need to be buried in her again.

Turning her over, I pull up on her hips gently and support her while she adjusts herself to her hands and knees. I don't miss a beat before sinking deep inside of her, and set a punishing pace. Grabbing at her hair, I fist her hair and tug her head up, turning it slightly so that I can see into my woman's eyes as I pound into her.

"Give me your eyes, Little Spitfire. I need to see those brown pools as you grip my cock with that pussy and milk every last drop of cum outta me." Tugging her hair, I last only a short while longer, before driving myself in as deep as I can and let myself explode inside of her. The pulsing from her own orgasm has me holding out on my own as long as possible.

Coming down from our shared pleasure, I move quickly to clean her up and get her tucked into bed, knowing that tomorrow will be a long day for us all. Needing to make sure that The Dungeon session Heather has set up runs smooth, the food for the wedding at the clubhouse goes off without a hitch, and that our woman has a good time at both.

Tucking Heather into her bed, I curl up behind her until I hear her breathing even out. Kissing her on the top of her head, I move slowly outta the bed, going to double checking on Sophie and even Sara before heading to the kitchen to call Country.

"Country, it's Bull. Have you found anything out about that BMW that was hanging around outside of here that night?"

"Unfortunately, yes Bull. Tank was able to track it down, and it's not good. The car belongs to Zack and from what Tank could come up with he has been hanging around for at least two weeks, stalking her every move."

Slamming my hand into the table, I quickly ask, "Why the fuck did we not know about this until now then, Country? She is obviously afraid of him taking Sophie from her, and we need to get in front of this shit, so that we can make sure our woman is safe."

"I know, I know Bull. We will need to sit down and talk with her about it. I was hoping that we would be able to wait until after the wedding, but I think it might be best to get her up early and get this shit over with" Pausing slightly, he goes on, "I wonder if this is the first time that he has reached out since she has moved? Maybe last week when she hurt herself he had reached out to her? Tomorrow morning, we will get her up and see what this man has over her, and we will come up with a plan to solve it. Then I'll give her a hand working on the food for the clubhouse tomorrow night. I know she has most of the shit all done, just needing to do a few last minute things."

"Yes, sounds good, Country. I can always help out plugging shit in or cutting shit up. Are you coming back here or heading home tonight?"

"I am heading back there now, I will be leaving Tank and Blaze's house momentarily, so I will be there in twenty minutes or so. What is our Spitfire doing? I can't wait to get home and sink deep inside of her."

"Well, unless you feel like waking her up, I would suggest maybe just snuggling in close to her and sleeping. I mighta worn her out, going a round or two after she laid Sophie down."

"Of course you did, you can never keep your dick outta our woman, especially when you are feeling a little anxious. Just as she can't keep the pain at bay when she feels the same way. When I get there I will send the prospect on his way, and we can take turns keeping watch tonight, if that's okay with you?"

"Yeah, that's fine, Country. I'm going to cuddle in next to our woman, you take the first shift outside." Hanging up before he can argue, I laugh to myself before heading upstairs and into the bed with our fiancé. Snuggling in close, I wait until I hear the rumble from Country's bike before letting myself drift off to sleep.

After Country dropped Sophie, Heather, and I off, I made sure to do a quick check through the house before we get Sophie situated for bed. I didn't see the BMW outside, but I know that fucker is probably around lurking in some fucking corner waiting to scare our girl even more. Fuck, why couldn't we have just gone over there that night we saw him and taken care of his fucking useless ass then? That would've put her worrying at ease, if nothing else. We don't need our girl stressed out seeing that she is going to have our baby.

OUR BABY! I can still barely believe it even after we made her take all the tests that I brought over to the house. After the fourth one she started really objecting, and I told her that we could keep the other six for the next few babies we have. The look on her face was priceless and the laugh that Country and I exchanged at her expense was something I can only hope we share many more of.

Seeing the way she is with Sophie, I know that we will have to work hard to keep up with how great of a mother she is. At least there will be two of us so maybe we would be able to have a fucking fighting chance.

As Heather gets Sophie ready for bed with a bath, I make sure to reach out to a few of the brothers setting up the work that we will need to get done over the next few days so we can get our home in order before we move our girls in next weekend. We will focus all our energy on Sophie's room and also the master suite and then if there is time the other rooms.

Grams and Country's Ma is so excited at the news of not only our upcoming wedding but the little one that will be joining our family. I think back to my days growing up with five brothers and sisters and know that I would love nothing more than a large family to grow older with. I grab my phone outta my pocket and decide it is past time to call my mom and dad to fill them in on what has been happening these last few months.

Hearing it ring only twice before my mom picks up I wonder where they are at. "Johnathan, my gosh are you alright? We haven't heard from you in so long, your brothers and sisters have said that you have found yourself a girl and that it's pretty serious. That you and Wayne finally found a woman that you could share between the two of you, that will be able to handle you both. Is that why you're calling us? To let us know that you have finally found the one that you are going to bring home to us? Don't make me call Wayne's Gram or Ma for that matter"

"Jesus Christ Ma, take a breath. Yes, Heather is it for us and yes, I will bring her by as soon as I can to meet the family. Not the only reason I was calling though. She has a daughter named Sophie that you will be happy to learn has decided to call us both daddy, so that means you will be a Grams yourself. Well, and the fact that Heather is pregnant as well."

"Johnathan, Oh honey, we are so happy for you that you are finally finding a family up there for yourself, we were all worried that the Club might not have been enough." She must pull the phone away from her because her next words are somewhat quieter, "Arthur, Johnathan is on the phone and he has some wonderful news to share." Getting louder, she speaks again, "Honey your daddy will be right on, please call and let me know when you and Wayne will be down here with your girls, and of course when you will be planning this big day. Here's your daddy now. I love you. Don't be so long in talking with us the next time please."

Taking a breath, I don't know how my dad gets a word in edgewise with her most the time. As I steady myself, my dad gets on the line, "Son, it's good that you finally called, your mom and I were just starting to worry that we haven't heard from you in a while. Been busy up there I hear from what your mom says huh? Got a little one on the way and a wedding in the works, seems to me that you mighta done that a little backwards, my boy, but as long as it gets done I guess that's what matters."

"Thanks Pops. We will all be moving into Wayne's house by next weekend and I was wondering if you thought maybe Christopher and Joseph would be able to come up and help out during the week?"

"I don't see why not, I will talk to them about it during dinner tonight, and find some coverage on the schedule for them during the week. It's a slow time for us as you can well remember so it shouldn't be a problem."

"Ok, I will get them plane tickets as soon as you give me the go ahead. Thanks for letting them outta work Pops, you know I wouldn't ask if I didn't need their help."

"I know you wouldn't boy. It's not like you call all the time like those sisters of yours having them rush about to hang a fucking picture for them."

Laughing at the thought of Angela and Jessica calling for just that dies in my throat the moment I see Heather walk into the room, with nothing except lust in her eyes. "Pops, my girl just came in, so I'm gonna let you go. Call me after you talk to the twins and please give me at least a day to get the tickets for them to get up here."

"Yea, yea son I will. Tell your girl congratulations from us, and that we are looking forward to meeting her and welcoming her into our family."

Disconnecting the call, I toss the phone across the bed, as Heather steps up between my legs, dropping to her knees before I can say a word. The moment her hands reach for my belt, I know that the discussion that I was going to have with her about my family, is going to wait. Because once her hands are on my flesh I am fucking done for.

No words are exchanged between us, as she pulls my cock free. The moment our flesh touches, my dick hardens in her hand, before her mouth is even close to it. Once it is, my dick throbs and pulses its need. As she swallows me down, I cannot stop myself from tangling my fingers into her hair and putting a little pressure on her head. The feeling of her gaging on my cock, only drives me on to wanting more and wanting to go deeper inside or her.

As the tears start to fall from her eyes, I know that I should be worshiping her, instead of treating her as nothing more than my whore, but I can't stop myself. The first time that I feel her swallow around my cock I know that this will not be lasting much longer. The second time she does it I feel my balls start to tingle and tighten. As she swallows one last time, my cock erupts and I growl out, "You take it all, Little Spitfire. You take what I will give you and you swallow it all down, like the good girl that you are. "

As she pops my cock outta her mouth, and looks up at me with those big brown eyes, I am fucking lost for a moment into the feelings I have for her. Scooping her up into my arms, I take her mouth with my own, and can taste myself mixing with her and am instantly hard again. Straddling my hips, I pull her skirt up before moving her panties to the side and sinking deep inside of her.

"Ride me, Spitfire. Make yourself come all over my cock, before I turn your ass over and fuck you on your hands and knees." Putting my hands under her ass, I help to lift her up as she bounces on my cock. After about two minutes, I reach around and stick a finger in her ass before her orgasm takes over her. And I have to bite my cheek to hold off the orgasm that is threatening to push me over."

Cuddling into me, I let her orgasm slowly fade before picking her up and laying her gently on the bed. Kissing her deeply, I make sure to go slowly as I kiss over every inch of our woman's body. I am not sure how we haven't noticed the small changes to her in these last few months but we haven't. I guess we are always too busy trying to bury ourselves inside of her and bring ourselves off to notice

146

the slight changes. The swell of her stomach, the darkening of her nipples, and the sensitivities that are starting to make themselves known as well.

Spending a lot of time on her stomach, I worship our baby and the area that he or she is growing in. Never, would I have thought I would feel such joy at such a thing, but I do. Just like the happiness that I find as her ring glitters in the light and I see the smile on her face as she looks to her hand. Seeing her hand move to her breast, I notice the ring as she is tugging at her nipples, and my cock gets painfully harder. Enough of this, I need to be buried in her again.

Turning her over, I pull up on her hips gently and support her while she adjusts herself to her hands and knees. I don't miss a beat before sinking deep inside of her, and set a punishing pace. Grabbing at her hair, I fist her hair and tug her head up, turning it slightly so that I can see into my woman's eyes as I pound into her.

"Give me your eyes, Little Spitfire. I need to see those brown pools as you grip my cock with that pussy and milk every last drop of cum outta me." Tugging her hair, I last only a short while longer, before driving myself in as deep as I can and let myself explode inside of her. The pulsing from her own orgasm has me holding out on my own as long as possible.

Coming down from our shared pleasure, I move quickly to clean her up and get her tucked into bed, knowing that tomorrow will be a long day for us all. Needing to make sure that The Dungeon session Heather has set up runs smooth, the food for the wedding at the Clubhouse goes off without a hitch, and that our woman has a good time at both.

Tucking Heather into her bed, I curl up behind her until I hear her breathing even out. Kissing her on the top of her head, I move slowly outta the bed, going to double checking on Sophie and even Sara before heading to the kitchen to call Country.

"Country, it's Bull. Have you found anything out about that BMW that was hanging around outside of here that night?"

"Unfortunately, yes Bull. Tank was able to track it down, and it's not good. The car belongs to Zack and from what Tank could come up with he has been hanging around for at least two weeks, stalking her every move."

Slamming my hand into the table, I quickly ask, "Why the fuck did we not know about this until now then Country? She is obviously afraid of him taking Sophie from her, and we need to get in front of this shit, so that we can make sure our woman is safe."

"I know, I know Bull. We will need to sit down and talk with her about it. I was hoping that we would be able to wait until after the wedding, but I think it might be best to get her up early and get this shit over with" Pausing slightly, he goes on, "I wonder if this is the first time that he has reached out since she has moved? Maybe last week when she hurt herself he had reached out to her? Tomorrow morning, we will get her up and see what this man has over her, and we will come up with a plan to solve it. Then I'll give her a hand working on the food for the clubhouse tomorrow night. I know she has most of the shit all done, just needing to do a few last minute things."

"Yes, sounds good Country. I can always help out plugging shit in or cutting shit up. Are you coming back here or heading home tonight?"

"I am heading back there now, I will be leaving Tank and Blaze's house momentarily, so I will be there in twenty minutes or so. What is our Spitfire doing? I can't wait to get home and sink deep inside of her."

"Well, unless you feel like waking her up, I would suggest maybe just snuggling in close to her and sleeping. I mighta worn her out, going a round or two after she laid Sophie down."

"Of course you did, you can never keep your dick outta our woman, especially when you are feeling a little anxious. Just as she can't keep the pain at bay when she feels the same way. When I get there I will send the prospect on his way, and we can take turns keeping watch tonight, if that's okay with you?"

"Yea, that's fine, Country. I'm going to cuddle in next to our woman, you take the first shift outside." Hanging up before he can argue, I laugh to myself before heading upstairs and into the bed with our fiancé. Snuggling in close, I wait until I hear the rumble from Country's bike before letting myself drift off to sleep.

CHAPTER
SIXTEEN

HEATHER

Waking up in the morning, the first thing I notice is the stiff cock nestled in the crack of my ass, and a lazy hand tracing circles on my belly. Taking a deep breath, I can smell Country in bed with me, and wonder at which point my men traded places with each other. Reaching my hand toward his, I grab for his fingers and that is when I catch the glimpse of my ring in the light and a smile comes to my face.

Feeling his breath in my ear, in a throaty voice he grumbles out, "Spitfire, I need to be buried deep inside of you." Feeling his fingers slowly stroke their way down to my pussy, he grabs onto my inner thigh bringing it up and over his hip, opening me wide for him. Beginning to play lazily with my pussy, he keeps discussing the events of the day as if his fingers were not touching me there, and bringing me to the edge of bliss. "We will eat breakfast before talking about this ex of yours. Then we will come up with some answers, before getting all the food heated up and over to the wedding this afternoon."

Moaning out, I am at a loss for what I am actually saying, and also as to anything that he might be saying. Nodding my head in agreement, I am not even sure what could need discussion at this point, but I really just want him to sink into me and fuck me. Why is he still talking?

"Spitfire, did you just zone me out there? What on Earth is more important than my fingers on you? Do tell me, please." slapping my pussy sharply, I shake myself outta my thoughts as he resumes his slow torture of my pussy.

"Yes, sorry Master. I was just wondering what on Earth you could be talking about, while I was feeling so near craziness with your fingers touching me, I just couldn't focus on what you were saying. I'm sorry."

Tsking at my absentmindedness, "I was talking about your safety, and the safety of our family, Heather. Once I have cum inside of you, we will talk about this with Johnathan and we will come up with a plan. Don't think that you can lie to us about this, or try to hide anything from us, like you did the last time we tried to speak with you about Zack." Squeezing my thigh tightly, he draws a gasp of shock outta me before going on, "You will tell us everything that we need to know to keep our family safe."

Feeling his hand slip away, I can imagine him grabbing his cock teasing it through my dripping wet pussy before burying himself to the hilt. Placing his hand on my hip, he drives into me with such force that I almost roll onto my stomach, the hand on my hip being the only thing stopping me. Gripping me tighter, he continues his assault until he is burying himself deep, leaving his load buried inside of me.

As we make our way outta bed, I head into the bathroom to shower and get ready for the day. Walking into the kitchen after I have dressed, I see Wayne and Johnathan both getting breakfast together. Looking around the kitchen, I move the few steps towards the living room, not seeing Sophie there I start to panic before arms are wrapped around me and Bull is in my ear, "She is next door with Irene and Preach. We need to talk and Sophie doesn't need to be here to hear what we need to talk about. We will go next door and pick her up when we are done. Then we will have the afternoon together to finalize the food for the dinner at the clubhouse before we head to the wedding. "Come on, let's have breakfast before we start."

Walking back into the kitchen, I am again greeted with the smells of bacon and coffee, both which make me so happy. Reaching for the coffee pot, my hand is quickly shooed away before I am able to grab the pot, forcing my eyes up to meet Wayne's. "What the hell, Wayne? I want some coffee, why are you shooing me away? Just let me get a cup before I sit down and we get this started."

"No, Heather, you can't have the caffeine," striding towards the stove, he picks up a cup and hands it to me. "I made you some decaf before I brewed the other pot, cream and sugar, just the way you like it. Sit, let's eat." Johnathan places a plate down in front of me, as I sit on the table, they sit on either side of me. Eating my fill, I throw the napkin down on my plate, and make my way to stand but I'm held tight in my chair with a hand on each arm.

"I'll get that for you, Spitfire, and Bull will get you some more coffee before we begin." Wayne is up and outta his seat before he finishes talking. Picking the dishes up from the table and setting them in the sink, Johnathan is up getting the carafe of coffee, refilling my cup.

Settling themselves back around the table, I look from one to the other and am not sure how to begin. As if he was reading my mind, Johnathan tells me, "Just start at the beginning with him, darlin'. We don't know much other than his name and the little that Tank has been able to dig up, so just start at the beginning and tell us as much as you can. Any and everything that you can think of will help, so that we know what we are dealing with."

Taking a deep breath, I steady my nerves before beginning the tale of me and Zack. How he was the starting quarterback on our school's football team, and in medical school studying to be a doctor. The story of how he pursued me for six long months before I eventually gave in to his constant attentions. How after that first date things between us moved quickly, losing my virginity to him only a few short weeks after that first date.

"After the first year that we were together, I started to notice a change in myself, I needed more out of the sex. We had always had a decent relationship, so I wasn't scared to tell him that I needed more. I mean, I had a hard time, because I wasn't even sure what it was that I needed. But, after some time and a little internet research, I was able to better put into words exactly what it was that I needed." Laughing to myself, I remember that first talk with Zack, "When I first brought it up, Zack thought it might be fun to slap my ass a little during sex." Shaking my head at the memory, "Except it wasn't, he didn't do it enough! Didn't do it hard enough, long enough, rough enough, just not enough." Looking from Johnathan to Wayne I smile wide before speaking, "We all know what a pain slut that I am. What he did to me really only pissed me off and drove me on to want more. I tried talking with him a few more times over a few months and I never was sated by what he would try."

Wringing my hands together under the table, I glance down at them before moving them up to the table. Each of my men grab up one of the hands in his own, and starts rubbing small circles into them, putting my mind at ease to the point that I would continue.

"He started treating me different then, and I knew that my needs were not lining up with his. I knew that I should have gotten outta there, but when I found out that I was pregnant, that didn't seem like an option for me any longer." Remembering again that time, I look up at both men, "My mood swings and hormones were all over the place being pregnant, so that's something that you guys can look forward to over the next few months." Smiling slightly trying to ease the tension that I feel, I wiggle a little in the chair as Wayne reaches for me.

"Spitfire, we look forward to all the experiences we will go through with you during this pregnancy. The mood swings, the weird foods, the doctor's appointments- "

Before he can go on, Johnathan cuts in waggling his eyebrows, "The increased sex drive."

Laughing out loud at his crassness, I have to remember where I was in the story before I can continue on. "After being with him three years, the last year when I was pregnant, Zack cheated more than a few times. He would call me names and fucking walk out the door when I would try to ask for pain during sex, making me feel like I was the fucking degenerate, even though he was the fucking degenerate. I suffered through that until the night that Soph came into my life. He was fucking someone the night that I went into labor for fuck's sake. I walked in on her fucking blowing him off in our guest room when I was going to ask him for a ride to the hospital."

Shaking my head at the memory, the men on either side of me are shaking their heads in understanding at the shit I went through during my first pregnancy. Wayne is the first to speak, "Heather, we will be here the whole time, and you will be sick of us hanging around and being as protective as I have a feeling that we will be."

"I know that, Wayne, I do. I know that neither of you would ever leave me alone to suffer through this pregnancy. I know how much you both want this baby and want for us to be a family." Leaning into Wayne first, I wrap him up in my arms, kissing him deeply before pulling away and getting wrapped up in Johnathan.

"While I was in the hospital I came up with a game plan that was only pushed on by Zack coming to visit us only one time in the three days I was there, staying for no more than fifteen minutes. Can you believe that shit? I don't even know if he ever held his daughter, I was still so outta it with some of the pain meds that I was on, but I do remember my heart breaking at that point. What kind of man would do that?"

Taking another deep breath, I go on, "I settled back into somewhat of a routine after I was released from the hospital, it didn't take long for me to know I needed a plan, especially when Zack let me know that me and the baby were nothing but a burden. I had everything planned out and he stopped me, said that I couldn't leave him. That me and that baby were his and no one would ever leave him. He didn't have a problem telling me how he would take her away if I ever left him, and it scared me enough that when I ran it was in the middle of the night, I knew better than to look back."

Taking a long sip from my coffee before I finish, "That's when I took off to New Orleans, and hooked up with Ember and Sara eventually. I found a guy that helped with domestic abuse survivors that needed to work off the grid."

"That's how you, Ember, and Sara were so well hidden for so long?" Johnathan looks at me saying.

"Yes, and that's how Ember and I were able to get our degrees as well. After Ember came back up with Vincent when her dad got sick, Sara and I didn't think there was a shot in hell that she would stay up here." Shaking my head at the memories, "When she finally told us she was staying I wished her well, and thought nothing of it or moving to Chicago, until the text I found from Zack. I left with little more than a suitcase and Sara's address the next day."

"I don't know how he found me so much quicker this time. I didn't think he would still be looking, but I guess he was. I heard from one of the girls at Club Coquin last week that he has been in there sniffing around lately." Dropping my eyes to the table, I start playing with the edge of a napkin that I find there before going on. "I am sorry that this is happening now. I know that we were just starting to get our own shit together as a family, I would understand if you wanted to stop- "

"NO!" comes out harshly from both of them in unison. Then Johnathan speaks, "We are in this together, Heather, no one will ever scare us away from you." Only supported by Wayne's words, "No one will ever take what is ours away from us."

The men each take turns pulling me into a tight hug before kissing me passionately. Then, they leave me to my kitchen and getting all the food situated for the party. Most of it I had already made and stored in the clubhouse kitchen in slow cookers or going on the pit, with a little help from Preach. The only things I needed to throw together this afternoon were some of the appetizers. Thankfully, I was able to get a cake made on short notice from a local bakery and knowing Ember, I got it in as many flavors as possible.

Two hours later, I am finishing up the food and call out to Johnathan and Wayne to help me pack up the truck. Having to search through the house, I find myself worried when neither of them or Sophie answers my calls. Moving out the front door, I find them both playing in the yard with Sophie and instantly my worries subside.

"Guys, I need your help loading up the car and getting this food over to the clubhouse. We need to have it all set up before the ceremony begins, even before Doc surprises Ember with the ceremony. Sophie, why don't you come on inside and get in the bath, then I will curl your hair and get you ready for the ceremony, before its Momma's turn to get ready."

"Momma, do I get to wear that pretty dress that we picked out last week?"

"Yes, baby, and you will get to play with Iris, Rose and Vincent as well." Getting up quickly, Sophie runs into the house and I remember how close her and Vincent were in New Orleans. I always knew that they would be trouble together and that theory has been proven true on more than one occasion. Looking towards my men, I let them know that the items in the kitchen need to be packed up and taken to the clubhouse. They let me know that the prospect will be over in a few and he would love nothing more than to load the van up and deliver the food safely to the clubhouse.

Johnathan's smile consumes his face as he steps closer to me. Leaning into me his voice rasps as he asks, "Will you be needing any help getting ready for the wedding, Little Spitfire? I do love helping you shower, so just know if you are in need, I would like nothing more than to help you out."

Reaching out, I scrub a hand over his face, and smile slyly. "Master, I would like nothing better, but I think that you and Wayne need to worry about your own showers after being out here all morning playing with Sophie." Turning quickly, I move into the house, heading up to the bathroom I start the water, throwing in a few toys and some bubble bath as the tub fills. Grabbing my phone, I make sure that the water is the right temperature before going down the hall to get Sophie. Stepping into her room, I see her on the phone as I enter.

"Sophie, sweetheart, who are you talking to?" stepping towards her, I see the fear in her eyes as she hands me the house phone. "Baby?" is all I get out before grabbing up the phone and putting it to my ear, "Hello?".

"I fucking told you, you dirty fucking slut. She. Is. Mine. If you run again, I will not only take her from you, but I will make it hurt, but not the kind that your little fucking freaky ass used to beg me for."

Slamming the phone down on the receiver, I check my expression before turning to Sophie and giving her a small smile.

"Was that Daddy?" she looks up at my saying in a whisper.

"That was the man that gave me what I needed to make you yes, sweetheart. But, your Daddies are those two men," pointing out the window, "out there. They will do everything to protect us from the man that gave me you, because he is not a nice man."

"I know Mommy, I remember the stories you would tell about him." Looking around the room, I think that she must have more questions, but she quickly changes her tune, "Can I take that bath now, Mommy?"

"Yes, of course Sweetheart," smiling at her innocence, "Let's get you all clean so we can get your hair all done, and that pretty dress on you." Taking a deep breath, I try to steady myself from the feelings that are running through me.

Moving into the bathroom, I again test the temperature before allowing Sophie into the tub. Pulling the curtain around her, I give her the privacy she often demands during her bath time, but sit close by on a chair in the hallway and proceed to lose my shit.

CHAPTER SEVENTEEN

BULL

Making my way upstairs to check on our girls, I stop short seeing the look in our woman's eyes as I pass by the bathroom. I wonder what the fuck happened in the past twenty minutes that we have been apart. Stepping closer to her, I lower my hand to her pulling her up and then further down the hall so we can talk.

Stepping into her room, I leave the door open so we can still hear Sophie in the tub. "What happened, Heather? You look like you have seen a ghost or something?"

Without meeting my eyes, she answers quietly. "After I got the bath water drawn, I walked into the room to get Soph, and she was talking on the phone with him."

"Him? Who are you talking about, Little Spitfire?" The venom in my tone, must serve as a warning to Heather, because her eyes shoot up to meet mine.

"Zack. I'm not sure what he was saying to her, if he even said anything at all, but when I took the phone from her to see who she was talking to, Zack was on the line spouting off."

"FUCK!"

Pulling her in tight, I reach for the phone in my pocket and shoot off a text to Prez, at the same time I am calling out for Country to get his ass upstairs. Pulling her into my chest, I let her know that there is nothing to be scared of. "Heather, you have nothing to worry about, he is probably just trying to get you riled up. I'm not sure why he called or what he said to Sophie, we will find him and make sure this shit doesn't continue." Pausing only briefly, I hold her even tighter before I see Country coming up the stairs.

"Country we have a situation. It seems that Zack decided now was a good time to reach out to our girls." Country looks from me to Heather and back as I go on, "he was on the phone with Sophie when Heather came up to put her in the tub."

"FUCK!" comes out harshly as Country moves closer towards us, taking our girl in his arms between us. Stroking over her hair lightly he asks, "What did he say to you, Spitfire?"

"I am not sure what he said to Soph, but he just told me that he wanted Sophie."

Grabbing her chin tightly, I lift her eyes up to my own and speak slowly, "Little Spitfire, don't start this out like that. Tell us exactly what he said to you on the phone we need to hear the words."

Rolling her eyes at us, she begins, "He called me a dirty slut, told me that Sophie was his and if I run away from him again he wouldn't only take her away from me, but he would make it hurt. And not the freaking kind of hurt that I like. That's when I hung up on him, and Soph asked me if it

162

was the Dad that gave her to me. I told her that you two are her real Daddies, and that you will do everything in your power to protect us from him, because he is not a nice man."

"Don't think on it Heather," Country says rubbing small circles into her back. "Today is a day for celebrating Ember and Doc's wedding. Finish up getting Sophie and yourself ready, I think that you have a date with Bull in the shower. Then we'll head over to the clubhouse."

Taking turns, we both kiss our girl with a passion and protectiveness that we have not needed to feel until this exact moment. Letting her leave the room before I turn and speak quietly to Country. "That was a fucking ballsy move he made, Country. He is really escalating this shit quick. I know that we only saw him for the first time yesterday, but this shit needs to be put to rest now." Nodding his head in agreement, I go on, "I let Prez know and I think we need to have someone on both of them twenty-four seven, until this shit is taken care of. What do you think, brother?"

"I agree brother; we will be with them at the clubhouse tonight, so we will just need to have a few prospects on the kids when they go over to Irene's after the ceremony, when the party really picks up." Looking towards the hall and then back at me, "Let's make sure we talk with Preach as well, so he understands what the hell is going on."

"I will head over to the clubhouse early and talk with him, and then shoot over to The Dungeon to make sure that Shadow and security over there have an eye out for him as

163

well." Scrubbing a hand down and over my face, I know that this shit is only going to get worse before it gets better. "I wonder how Zack fucking found her so quick this time. It took him all of five years to find her the last time, and now all of a sudden she has been up here for less than a year and he has eyes on her already. That seems a little fucking shady to me, wonder who the fuck he has in his pocket to help him?"

"Yeah, I hadn't really thought of it like that, but now that you say that I agree. He must have found someone with a grudge or something, because she hasn't been straying too far from the way she lived in New Orleans as far as I could tell."

Hearing a noise, we both look towards the bathroom, and see Heather still sitting on a chair outside the door, not making a fuss. Looking back towards Country, I ask, "Is there anyone that has a grudge against either of us? I can't think of anyone out of the ordinary, not since that shit with the Knights settled the hell down."

"No, the only shadows that I have are far in my past, and I don't think that they will come knocking on the door from Texas anytime soon." I know the shit that happened in Texas with his dad, but after all these years it couldn't matter anymore. Looking out the window over my shoulder, I turn to and see the BMW parked across the street again. Moving quickly, we both head for the front door, and are through it within only a few short seconds. Hitting the street, the BMW pulls away before we are able to reach it, the sound of the tires screeching being muffled by our voices yelling out.

"Bull, whatever this piece of shit wants we are gonna need to put it to rest. There is no way that he is going to get Sophie, and I think he might have plans for our Little Princess as well. One of us is with her at all times, unless we have Church, and maybe we should lay low for a while? The clubhouse is probably the safest place for us, for the time being."

"There is no fucking way that Heather will stay at the clubhouse with Sophie, Country. And I for one, am not going to fight with her about it, she has barely just settled in to being ours, to having us own her pleasure and pain, I don't want her trust in us thrown to the wayside. I think if one of us is with her at all times, and we get the prospects to watch over her from a distance as well that should be good."

"Ok, but if this shit escalates then we are doubling the watch. She is pregnant with our fucking kid and there is nothing that I won't do to keep her safe. She will not go through this pregnancy and birth like she did with Sophie, alone and miserable. No matter what we need to do to make her happy. Yes?"

"Agreed," Making our way back into the house, I know that I will not be leaving until the prospect is here to help watch out for this fucking asshole. Looking at Country I feel the tension between us, needing to push that shit down I say, "You are walking our girl down the aisle tonight, so I think it's only fair that I am the one that gets to play with her at The Dungeon. That sound good to you?"

Hitting me on the arm his answer is firm, "No asshole. That doesn't sound good to me, you want to walk her down the fucking aisle Bull, you go the fuck ahead. I didn't volunteer for that shit, that was all Sara's doing." Stopping near the top of the stairs he goes on after thinking to himself for a while. "I thought that I would never be walking down a fucking aisle for Doc, and now we are going to have to start planning our own fucking wedding soon."

"I know brother. We didn't even know her a year ago and here we are, with a kid on the way and ready to settle the fuck down." Looking around the kitchen, I grab up some left over breakfast before adding, "Country, I talked with my Mom and Pops and they are letting the boys come up next week to help with the remodeling, if they want. I told Pops I would get them plane tickets to come up as soon as he gave the word that he could get them off the schedule. So, if this shit with her isn't handled by then we will always have Frick and Frack to help out."

"Come on, that's almost like more of a chore than a help. Joseph and Christopher are what, pushing eighteen now? They will probably just be chasing pussy the whole time they are here."

"Nah, they are going to be twenty, next month. If they come, they will be here to work and the shit will get done a hell of a lot quicker with the two of them around. They have been working at Pops company since they were fucking fifteen, so these few repairs and improvements that we want will be nothing for them." Looking around the house, I go on, "I'm sure they wouldn't mind if we took them to the clubhouse for a party or two, but with Zack on the loose they will fucking understand our need to lay low."

Hearing a bike pull up outside, I glance out the window to see the prospect sitting on his bike. "Well, after I step in the shower with our girl I am off to check on the set-up at the clubhouse and The Dungeon. If I run into Prez or Tank I will talk with them more about this situation, and I'll call if I find anything out. Otherwise, I'll see you guys at the clubhouse for the wedding."

Striding from the room, I take the stairs two at a time, reaching the bathroom quickly. Knocking on the door, Heather opens it quickly. Noticing that Sophie has left the bathroom and our girl is naked, I pull her into my arms, kissing her deeply. Moving away, I head towards the shower and turn the water on. Making sure the water is right, I bring our girl over, and help her into the shower before loving on her body. As I am drying her off, I kiss her again on the hair and let her know, "I'm off to double check everything, Little Spitfire. See you at the clubhouse for the ceremony." Pulling away I make my way out the house and next door to talk with Irene quick. Seeing Preach's bike outside, I know that he will be there tonight to help keep an eye on the kids, which helps put my mind to ease. Knocking on the door, I hear arguing before Preach opens the door staring daggers at me.

"What the fuck do you want, Bull?" he says stepping out of the house, pulling the door closed behind him. "I thought you would be at the clubhouse getting the shit in order for the wedding tonight."

"Yeah, I'm on my way over there, but I had to stop and talk with you and Irene first." Looking between him and the closed door, "You okay brother?"

Looking at his watch, he shakes his head saying, "Same shit different century brother. Tell me what you need to and get your ass moving or your gonna be late."

"I'm not sure if Prez told you but, Heather's ex has come back into the picture and has been threatening her and saying he is going to take Sophie away. I don't know- "

Cutting me off the door slams open, and I see Irene step out onto the porch with us. "That piece of shit needs to stay the fuck away from those girls." Looking between me and Preach she goes on, "He never treated Heather very well and he only wants that poor little girl to fuck with her Momma." Turning to Preach, she leans into him putting a hand on his chest, "You're not going to let that man hurt those little girls are you?"

"No, of course not Momma," I don't miss the eye roll that Irene does at this name as Preach goes on, "no matter what goes on between us, I would never let anyone hurt one of your girls you love so much." Nodding towards him, she turns quickly on her heel and heads back into the house. I am not sure what the fuck is going on between these two, but obviously they have a hell of a past that nobody knows about.

"Preach, are you planning on being here with her and the kids tonight or are you staying at the clubhouse after the ceremony?"

"I was planning on coming back here, and helping Irene and Grams out with the kids after dinner. I guess with this ex of Heather's on the prowl, I won't be the only one keeping eyes on them, right?"

"No, Prez has a few prospects on it and I just wanted to reach out and make sure that if you were here you would know the score. Of course, it would put mine and Country's mind at ease knowing we had a little extra security with you being here as well."

"No worries, brother. I got you in this, go have fun with your girl and don't worry about the kids, we will handle it, and no one will get near them."

Clasping his arm, "Thanks brother. See you at the ceremony."

Walking to my bike hoping that tonight goes off without any hiccups, I am quick to get this show on the road and see our girl in between us again.

CHAPTER EIGHTEEN

COUNTRY

Seeing how freaked out she was when Bull called me upstairs, let me know that this shit with her ex is really wearing on her. That shit can't be good for the baby, but I know that once we get our hands on Zack, his ass will not be scaring our girl anymore. We just gotta catch up to him, before he makes another move against her.

Moving towards the bathroom, I hear Heather and Sophie talking from inside and lean against the wall to listen.

"Momma, why did he call to talk to me today?"

"Sophie, I am not sure why he called."

"I thought that you always told me that he was a bad man, Momma? He didn't seem like such a bad man, Momma."

Feeling my heart break, I am about to open the door, when my woman's words stop me.

"Baby, that man has never been a father to you. He gave you to me, yes, but that is all he did for us. Giving you to me was by far the best thing that he has ever done in his life, Baby. The men that have asked momma to marry them, that have asked you for your permission to be their little girl, that have asked for you to be in their lives, those

170

are the men that should be in our lives, should be my husbands, should be your daddies, not the man that was on the phone with you. That man is trying to take you away from me, because he is not a nice man."

"I know Momma. I know that Papa Johnathan and Daddy Wayne are the ones who should have always been with us. The way they look at you and the way that you have talked about them let me know that. I just wished that we could have found them earlier. You have been sad for so long Momma; I just wish that you would have found them sooner because you're happy now."

Hearing the catch of breath from Heather, I know what her daughter has said must have forced tears from her gorgeous eyes. Opening the door, I see them embracing each other and scoop them up into my arms, hugging them tight to me.

"We were meant to be together and I wish that we could have found you sooner as well, Little Princess. Papa and I will do our best to make sure that nothing ever comes between us from here on out." Stroking along Sophie's tear stained cheek, I go on, "If there is anything that we could hope we could have changed, it would be that, Princess. Your Momma is something that neither Papa Johnathan nor I will ever do without again."

Staying there wrapped around Heather and Sophie, does nothing to lessen the fear I feel thinking about Zack and his plans for them. Knowing the time is getting late, I pull away slowly and let the girls know that they need to finish getting ready because, "This wedding isn't going to wait for us."

Leaving them to finish getting themselves ready, I grab my clothes out of my bag and wait for them to leave the bathroom so I can grab a quick shower. Throwing on my long sleeve shirt, I feel odd putting my cut on over it, but know this is how Doc would like their wedding to be. I must say that I am really looking forward to the scene that Heather has worked out for Ember and Pearl after the ceremony at The Dungeon. Watching those two women together is certainly something. But, in reality I am looking forward to claiming our woman together tonight. The first time since we have put our ring on her. We have gone easy on her these last months, only taking her together on a few occasions, knowing how difficult it might be for her. Tonight that will fucking change. Tonight Johnathan and I will bury ourselves in our woman as she comes undone around us and she will know who she belongs to.

Throwing on my boots, I head towards the kitchen, and don't have to wait long, before I am greeted by two beauties. Sophie looks sweet in her little frilly dress, while Heather looks ready to be out of the red bridesmaid dress she has on. She looks absolutely breathtaking in the dress, don't get me wrong, but it is not her style, causing her to be uncomfortable, which I don't like. Walking towards her, I scoop her up in my arms, snuggling into her ear I whisper, "Spitfire, you look breathtaking, I can't wait to get you to The Dungeon tonight, so Johnathan and I can peel that dress off of you, tan your ass up some, and be buried deep inside of you together."

Feeling the heat rise to her cheeks I know my speech has given her some added comfort. Pulling back, I add, "Johnathan will love this dress on you, red is such a special color to him for you. It's the color of the tattoo that he is having done for you."

"Tattoo, what tattoo?" she says looking up at me with wide eyes.

"Shit," Looking towards Sophie, "Sorry Sophie, I shouldn't have said that." Looking back towards Heather I go on, "We are each having a tattoo added for you, and when you are ready Gun will do one for you as well. I forgot that Bull and I hadn't talked to you about it yet, but it was something that we have planned since the day we picked up the rings."

Smiling slightly, she leans up into me, running her fingers through my beard. "I love you," adding on a whisper in my ear so Sophie doesn't hear, "Master." And with that my cock is rock hard.

FUCK! It's going to be a long fucking night.

Pulling into the clubhouse a short while later, I let Heather go off to find the women and lead Sophie over by where the kids have all gathered. Watching the kids for a bit, I remember when this shit, kids and a woman were the furthest thing from my mind. Moving back towards the bar, I order myself a beer and am taking a swig as Tank, Bull, and Doc park their asses next to me.

"Congrats, brother. I'm glad you and Ember are finally tying this shit down, six years and you have finally caught her, huh? But, really, I had to wear this fucking dress shirt for this shit?"

"Just wait man, you think shit is crazy now, wait until your ol' lady is eight and a half months pregnant and if you tell her no, she will just fucking start bawling. Or when she's sending you out on ice cream and pickle runs at fucking two in the morning. See how long you two are going to be able to keep saying no to that shit." Doc says taking a swig from his beer. Leaving the beer resting near his lips he adds, "Fucking woman!" before tipping the bottle back and taking another swig.

Toasting this man, Tank, Bull, and I raise our beers up to him. Enjoying another beer with these men, the mood around us slowly changes and I realize it's time for the ceremony to start. Moving to the back of the clubhouse, I wait for Heather to come out so I can walk her down the aisle. As I wait my mind wanders again to the woman that has captivated me so. Thinking about the way she snuggles into my neck as she is cumming around my cock. The way she moans out as Bull is buried deep inside her. Losing myself in the thoughts, the only thing that jars me outta my own head is a push from behind me. Looking behind me Gun is rolling his eyes, and pointing forward, "Get a move on, brother." Is all he is able to say before I am shaking my head outta the fog, looking up to see Heather standing in front of me waiting to start this little walk down the aisle.

Not wanting to waste another minute, I grab her arm up, and we slowly make our way down the aisle. Seeing Bull waiting off in the wings, I know that this shit is only practice for what is to come. Bull gives me a nod, and turns his full attention to our girl. Stopping next to Preach, I kiss our girl and head over to the side of Doc. As Ember slowly makes her way down the aisle with Little Vincent and Prez, I see the complete joy in her eyes and can only hope to make our Heather that same way always.

After dinner, we pack up the kids and get them over to Irene's house. We had to take three trucks to get all the kids over there, but between me, Tank, and Bull we were able to do it. I don't have any clue how Bull's parents did it with five kids, I am lucky if I can handle one or two, not to mention Rebel still being so little. I am not sure how this shit is going to work when Heather has our baby, but I know for damn sure, I am excited as fuck to see it through.

Setting up all the spare sleeping arrangements, we make sure that Preach, Irene and the two prospects outside are in need of nothing before heading off to the last stop of the evening. As we make our way to The Dungeon, we are greeted by Shadow at the back door. He pulls me aside, and lets me know that security has seen the BMW a few times this evening, and that he has additional men working in case anything was to happen.

Heading into the locker room, I take a deep breath as I am finally able to take this collared and cuffed shirt off. Pulling on my leathers, I feel much more at home and hope to fuck Heather doesn't want that shit or worse, a fucking tux, for our wedding. Moving back out towards the main floor, I catch up with Bull at the bar and wait for our girl to get her sweet ass out here by us.

Bull takes a swig from his beer before turning towards me, "Did you see the extra security around?"

"Yeah, they stick out like a sore thumb and Heather will definitely notice something, if we don't keep her mind and body occupied tonight." I say taking a long pull from my beer.

"That I don't have a problem doing, brother." Bull says on a laugh. I notice his eyes track towards the hallway, and see his mouth curve up in a smile, and know our woman is coming. Turning the stool slowly, I am met with a fucking vision. Heather is wearing an outfit that we got for her months ago. An outfit we were so scared to give her, because we didn't know if she would be able to handle the both of us, especially together.

The night we claimed her told us all we needed to know about her.

Walking into The Dungeon, I wipe my palms against my jeans, and can't believe that I am fucking scared for this shit. Bull and I have had this shit planned for well over a month, and I know that it will go off as planned, so why am I still so nervous? I know why, because the one thing I can't predict is our Spitfire. If she will be receptive to our idea, if our bodies call to hers, like hers does to us. If she will give us a shot to master those subtle curves of her body, and not just let us take her pain and pleasure. If she will submit to us in all things, and not run when we speak of building a future between the three of us.

Bull stopped by to set up the room earlier in the day, while I was running around getting the last minute shit. I had to stop off at the jewelry store and pick up the collar that we had made for our girl. She will fight us on it, I know she will, it is in her nature to be strong willed, and she has been alone for far too long. She needs us to help and take some of the burden off of her, even though she may not know it yet.

Moving towards the room that we have set aside for tonight, I unlock the door, and take a few steps inside. Moving towards the bed, I take out the box from my kit and lay it inside of the drawer of the nightstand. Moving towards, the other dresser, I grab out a pair of nipple clamps and a chain that will attach to her clit as well. Having our girl primed and ready by the time we bring her here will only add to our chances of getting her to be ours.

Hearing the door open, I glance towards Bull as he looks down at my hands and a grin takes over his face. "Good idea, Country, I was thinking much the same way, that our girl may need a little something to help her along tonight. Maybe that green plug as well? She did seem to enjoy it last time I had it buried inside her tight little asshole."

Laughing to himself he moves over to the nightstand and opens the drawer, pulling out the box I had just placed inside. Opening the box, he looks back towards me, "They really did do a wonderful job on this piece, Wayne. When we went in there, I knew right away by looking at some of the pieces they had around the store, that they would be able to handle our design ideas. Thank fuck that Prez gave us that guy's name." Scrubbing a hand over his face, he closes the box and turns towards me, "Does the ring look just as good?"

Smiling wide, I reach into my kit and pull out the smaller box, tossing it across the room to him. "It looks even better, if I do say so myself."

Popping the box open, and looking at the ring that we have had designed as well, he nods his head in agreement. "This we can wait on, for a little while at least. We both know how she has fought being with us. Getting our collar on her, will fucking help break her into the idea that we are not going anywhere, and that we will always be here when she needs us." Holding the box up, he tosses it back to me and as I tuck it back into my kit he adds, "but, soon that too will be on her flesh, just as our ink will be. Then she will never get the chance to run or fight these feelings we have again."

"True brother." Taking one last look around the room, "She's not here yet?"

"Nah, she was dropping Sophie off by Irene's when I left to come over here, she said she would be along in about fifteen minutes. Grab those clamps up brother and I will have Shadow hand them off to her with the clothing I have. Then meet me by the bar so we can wait for our girl."

Handing over the clamps and grabbing for the green plug, I move towards Bull, knowing that tonight is the first step to making this girl ours. We have talked about it at the clubhouse more often than not since the first night we met.

As we wait by the bar, I feel the change and know that our girl is near. Turning slowly, I slap Bull on the shoulder and as we look towards each other, the sight of our girl dropping down to her knees, is one that will never get old in my mind, even if she struggles with it so.

"Spitfire, you do us proud by agreeing to scene with us again tonight." Stroking a hand over her head, I notice the slight tension that leaves her body as my hand touches her.

As her head drops down, I look towards Bull and we know the struggle that is raging within our girl. Bull is the first to address the struggle that we see.

"Little Spitfire, we know how you feel about kneeling down to anyone, but here in this place, and when we are going to tear into you like we have planned for tonight, we will need you to show us the respect that we deserve. We are not asking you to be subservient to us, or even to be submissive at any other time, the only time we will ever ask you for it, or more so demand it from you, will be here. You may speak, I know that you are struggling, we only want you to be comfortable with us. Please tell us whatever your worries are."

Looking up towards us, I see only strength behind the eyes that are usually so lost, especially when she is in need of pain, like she is now. She speaks directly to us making eye contact the entire time, "I have no questions, I only want the pain that you two can give me. I will kneel down for you, seeing that is what you want, but know that it is not easy for me to do."

"Spitfire, we need to know that you are with us in this, that you will be able to be open and honest in all things. If we are going to show you the kind of pain that you need, you will need to show us, that you can respect us. Your kneeling

to us is that only, it is not as you have so often told me, 'Giving the power up.' We have all talked and you know that you have all the power, even when you are broken down and opened wide. It is always you." I say reaching out for our girl, pulling her up to her feet.

Squishing her between us, I am already hard, with thoughts of taking her together. "Come, lets watch a bit of Ember and Pearl before we head to our room." Following my lead, we walk our girl towards the main stage watching for only a brief time. Only being able to watch the two women for a short time, I can already smell my girl and am sure she is leaking down her leg, waiting for us to take her. I wait only moments before I look towards Bull and see the lust in his eyes as well. Each grabbing up one of our girl's arms, we make quick work of the distance to the room we have for the evening.

Bull and I have this night pretty much planned and we both know that we would like to start by getting our collar on our girl. Asking her to kneel on the pillow next to the bed, we move about the room getting the few things that we need.

As I walk towards our girl, I speak words that have been itching to be said since the moment we met. "Spitfire, we brought you here tonight, to ask you something. We have been dancing around this shit for weeks, and Bull and I would like to move further down this road we have been on with you."

"What Country means, Heather, is that we would like for you to wear our collar," reaching down he runs a finger

around her neck, "as much as you are comfortable with for now, if that is only you when we are here, or you when we are at home, or at the clubhouse, wherever you are comfortable. We know that soon we will be together in all ways as a family and we are willing to wait for you." Bull says stroking over our girl's neck.

Moving towards the nightstand, I grab the box out and move back towards our girl. Grabbing her hair up, Bull brings it off to the side, so that I can slide the collar into place. "This is the way that we will show our ownership of you, Spitfire. When you wear this collar, you will remember that we are your Masters, that we are the ones who own your pleasure and your pain. That we are the ones that will give you any and every thing that you want, need, and deserve." Fastening the necklace into place, I grab for her hands pulling her up to her feet again. "Tell us that you are ours, Heather. That we are the only ones that you will give yourself to. The only ones that you will give your pleasure to. The only ones that will give you the pain that you seek." I growl out as I pull her into my bare chest. Feeling her breath against my skin, my cock is fighting against the restraints of my pants.

"Spitfire, we need to watch you fly before we bury ourselves deep inside of you. Get your ass over to the cross and let me strip you down before I tie you up, and Bull has his way with you." Moving slowly, I guide her over to the cross, before slowly unzipping the green leather skirt and dragging it down her legs. As my hand skims back up her legs, I hear Bull groan from behind us and understand what he is feeling. Reaching her hip, I lightly trace a finger over the matching corset that she is wearing. Tightly at her hip, I spin her around, and am greeted with her lush ass filling my hand. Bending her over slightly, I can see the plug sticking out of her ass, and am fucking reminded that there are clamps on her breasts and clit. I slide my fingers over the plug and move them until they are resting on the clamp that is attached to her clit. A small groan escapes her lips as I touch and tug on the jewelry. "Oh Spitfire, how responsive you are, I would say even needy. I do hope you can handle the session that Bull has planned for you."

Pushing onto her back I have her bent over at almost a ninety-degree angle before, I drop to my knees, releasing the clamp that has been fastened to her clit for most of the evening. Hearing the sharp hiss from her lips, I lean in, taking her clit in my mouth soothing away the hurt that we have caused. The hiss turns into moans of pleasure within a short time, and I know our girl is ready for more.

After bringing her off, I get to my feet and finish taking off her clothing. The corset is easily dropped to the side, as I release one then the other nipple clamp, latching onto each nipple in turn to soothe the ache. Stepping back, I know that Bull is hungry to get his hands on our woman. And I leave him to his work trying not to think about the anguish these sessions cause in me. Each one is better than the last, but it still is not how I saw my life going.

As I pull myself outta these thoughts, I see that Bull has finished up with our girl and she is flying high. Helping him take her down off the cross, we move her slowly to the bed, before waiting on her to give us some signal of consciousness. As she comes back around, and comes *down from her flight, Bull and I are eager to move on with the claiming of our woman.*

Taking our time, we make sure that our girl is back with us 100% before we start our assault on her luscious curves. Leaving her on the bed, we roll her onto her back gently as to not disrupt the fresh welts that are forming on her back, ass, and thighs. Spreading her legs wide, Bull dives into our girl's pussy with fever. I sit back watching for a time, before I am drawn to her mouth by the moans spilling from it. Kneeling up on the bed, I brush a hand over her nipples and am rewarded with another groan that only drives me to bend down taking her nipple in my mouth. Sucking on her tit has me hard, and wanting to feel her lips wrapped around my cock. Crawling up the bed, she doesn't miss a beat as I free myself from my leathers, and sink into her mouth. Taking me deep has me groaning out saying, "Fuck me, Spitfire. Your mouth is like fucking heaven. Keep sucking my cock like that and I might come right down your throat instead of inside that hot tight cunt like I really want to. Bull, you need to give our girl a little reward for what she is doing to me with her mouth up her. Make her come and then let's bury ourselves deep in our girl and let her know who owns her."

Holding myself off, I am almost pushed over when I feel the vibrations from my girl's orgasm pulsing over my cock. As Bull pulls back from her, the sounds of her pleasure are fucking music to my ears. Looking down to where Bull is I see that our girl, our Spitfire, is squirting all over the bed as his fingers are still pumping inside of her. "Bull, who knew our girl had it in her to orgasm like that? I for one, am happy as hell to know that she has it in her and glad that you gave her that little treat before we are both balls deep inside of her."

Pulling myself out of her mouth, I move to the end of the bed, helping our girl to get up. The smile that tugs at Bulls mouth is one of pure joy knowing he will be buried in our girl within a few short moments. Lying on his back with his legs braced against the end of the bed, he grabs his cock stroking up and down it while taking in our girl's lush curves. "Come here, Little Spitfire, come sit on your Master Johnathan's cock."

With a smile on her lips our girl does just that, not pausing as she crawls the bed, swinging a leg over Bull, before impaling herself on his cock. Sinking all the way down, she slowly moves herself back up before repeating the process again and again. Hearing the moaning coming from her I know that I will not last long once I am inside of her. "Baby, I can't wait any longer. I need to bury myself in your ass, and claim you as ours and make that collar you are wearing mean so much more."

Moving to the bedside table, I am grabbing for the lube as the words she is saying register with my mind. "Fuck me Wayne, I don't need any lube, just fuck my ass like it belongs to you." Stepping away from the night stand, I am behind her in an instant. Slapping her ass, I hear her cry out as I pull her hair, bringing my mouth to her ear. "Your ass is ours, Spitfire, and there is nothing that you can do to stop us from claiming you together, right fucking now." And with that small warning, I bury myself deep inside her ass with no more than the precum on my cock as lube.

Feeling Bull's cock retreat from her cunt, I drive in deep and the tight grip her ass has on me is something that I will never forget. As Bull pushes back in, I draw myself out and the friction from our cocks must be driving our girl crazy. On my next thrust inside of her, our girl is tightening up and squeezing our cocks as she shatters. Grabbing her hips for leverage, it isn't long before we find our rhythm, and we are pounding into her with little or no thought between our strokes. We are both chasing our orgasms after what seems like only moments, as I feel the walls around her asshole shake with her orgasm Bull and I both lose the battle and erupt inside of her.

Tumbling to the bed, we wrap ourselves around her, one in front one behind, and doze off. Waking up about an hour later, we work in tandem to get our girl cleaned up and ready to leave. As we are walking her towards the door, I pull her into my arms as Bull steps behind her. "You are ours now, Spitfire. We will give you time to get used to it, and will not expect you to wear the collar at all times, yet, but you will come to us with any issues or problems that you have. We are the ones to give you your pleasure or- "

"I understand, Master Wayne. You and Master Johnathan are the ones that own me, I got it. You don't have to speak to me like I am- "

Reaching around her, Bull puts his hand over his mouth stopping her speech. "I wouldn't go on with those thoughts right now, Little Spitfire, we are only telling you what we demand of you. YOU. ARE. OURS."

That night started this whole thing, and it will live with all of us forever.

CHAPTER NINETEEN

BULL

Seeing the extra men throughout The Dungeon has set my mind at ease, somewhat. I know that neither Country nor I will leave our girl alone, but fuck it still hurts my soul to think that someone might get to her. Ever since the first night that we were both buried deep inside of her, I think that I have known I would never be without her. She has struggled over the weeks, but coming around and saying yes to our proposal has me knowing that her mind is right in step with our plans for our future, especially seeing that she is pregnant.

Lifting the beer to my lips, I feel her moving towards us, I sense her before I turn to see her coming. When I look to her and realize what she is wearing, I about came in my pants with the thoughts of the night we collared her, the night we first claimed her as our own. Every night that has followed has gotten us closer to this, closer to the one and only thing that I have strived for, my own family. As she bends down and kneels at our feet, her movements are so practiced and precise, I know that her every move is a representation of us, and that's what makes it so good that we have her, and that her struggle to obey us has all but disappeared. We don't want her hurt or worse if something happened with Zack, so her complying when we asked something is exactly what we need.

The scene that we have planned tonight is not for the faint of heart, and our girl is surely that. She has been stressed since the note and then the phone call. She relaxed for a while, during the ceremony at the clubhouse and it was good to see her smile. This relaxation is different, the peace that she will get from this session is different. I will tan her ass up nice with my whip, while Country can bury himself down her throat. Then we will take her together, but first our girl deserves to watch the scene she has set up for her friends.

Finishing the rest of our drinks, we move to our feet and both slip a hand under our girl's arm, helping her to her feet. As we make our way towards the stage, we hold our girl between us tightly, enjoying the feel of her between us. Finding a spot off to the side of the stage, I look across and see not only Ember's husband but both of Pearl's as well. Their eyes are trained on their women, who are in the midst of their scene, as ours slowly move over Heather. Seeing the small movements that she is making only makes my cock throb as more blood rushes to it. Rubbing her thighs together, she is trying her best to stave off the delicious ache that she is feeling. The ache that only Country and I can satisfy in her, and if she can't stop what she is doing, we will need our room quicker than any of us would like.

Running a hand down her back, I stop my movements, resting it gently on her ass. Moving closer to her ear, I squeeze her ass roughly as I growl out, "Stop your dirty movements, Little Spitfire. I can smell your desire from up here, and every time that your legs are rubbing together so hard, I bet your juices are leaking further down your leg. If you can't contain yourself, we will not be able to stay down here to watch this scene that you so painstakingly set up." Squeezing her ass harder, I add, "You wanna stay and watch your friends play, don't you?"

"Yes, please Master Wayne, Master Johnathan. I want to watch Ember and her Ma'am give each other pleasure, before you take yours from me." She whines, looking up at us under those long, luscious lashes. We both know that she chooses her words wisely, knowing what she has said will bring us to the edge of sanity.

"You, my Little Spitfire, are getting too big for your own britches," Country drawls out running a hand over her face, snagging her up by the scruff of her neck, pulling her into him roughly before taking her mouth with his. As he consumes her with the kiss, my cock knows only pleasure seeing how she bends to Country's demands. Running my hands over the green leather skirt, my mind trails back to the first night she had it on, and the way it was peeled off of her before we both took her. My mind thinks of that night frequently, the night we collared our girl and made her ours.

Palming my cock through my leathers, my eyes rake over our girl before going back to the scene in front of us. Watching Pearl, who looks like she has spent some time serving her Masters before coming here tonight, own Ember is really something special. The way they feed off of each other, and their Master's, is something that I see in Heather each night that we take her.

Letting this scene go for a while longer, we wait until Pearl has invited Doc up onto the stage to fuck his wife's throat before we make our exit. Taking our girl to the room that we have set up for our night, we have her stripped and restrained to the bed before long. Running a hand along her spine, I cannot help myself from sticking two fingers into her. Groaning at the wetness and heat that I find there, I can't stop myself from pumping into her as I take a knee behind her. Continuing the assault with my fingers, I lean in and inhale our woman's scent. A scent that it seems I can never get enough of.

Sticking my tongue out, I run it from my finger up and through her heat, until I reach her asshole. Tonguing her asshole, I scissor the fingers that I have buried deep inside her. "You were made for us, and I don't know how much longer I can wait to have us buried inside of you again." Burying my face into her again I find that about two minutes is all that I can last eating at my Little Spitfire, until the need of my cock outweighs the pleasure I am trying to bring our girl. Standing up, I pop my fingers out of our girl and see that Country is already naked, with his cock in hand waiting to take our girl.

Tossing my whip to me, he growls, "Do your worst to that ass, redden it up and those fat thighs of ours, as well brother, I am going to bury myself down her throat until I am coming. Then let's get her up off the bed and she can ride me, while you fuck that tight asshole we both love so much."

Moving to the bed, Country crawls the few steps until he slides his ass to a sitting position, right under our girls face. Her arms are bound out to her sides and the way he is sitting has her head bobbing on his dick in an instant. Seeing the look on his face and the ecstasy that takes over, has me needing to slow myself down or the strength of my whip will be too much, if that is even possible, for us. I have no wants to truly hurt our girl, even if that is something that she thinks she needs. The pleasure we take from her body after we give her the pain she desires, truly helps her flight. Flying is something that we expect from our woman every time we fuck now, ever since that first night. Much the same as her squirting out during her orgasms, at least once each time we take her. If she doesn't, we know where her head truly is, knowing that it is most likely not in the moment with us if she doesn't let loose enough to fly for us.

Standing back taking in this scene, I need to adjust myself again, before letting the whip unravel and snapping it to the side. The crack that rushes through the room, has a moan spilling from our girl's lips in anticipation and Country's head shooting up. Seeing the grin on his lips, he reaches for our girl's hair and digs his fingers into it, wrapping it around his fist driving himself deeper inside of her as I land the first lash. Moving from foot to foot, I alter my position slightly before cracking the whip off to the side again, and then landing it again across our girl's lush ass. Having her spread open before me as she is, only drives my need to mark her pale flesh more. Seeing the first two stripes coming to the surface of her skin, has me again shifting on my feet. Landing two more without much of a pause between them, I grin seeing the tension leave Heather's body as she relaxes back into position. Landing a total of five more before dropping the whip, with each strike she is that much closer to flying. On the tenth strike, I see Country coming undone, and know our girl will be swallowing his cum in seconds. Grabbing up the Spitfire paddle from the bedside table, I wait until the moment Country tenses, starting to explode down her throat before the paddle lands for the first time on her ass.

Knowing how nervous Country is when I am landing strikes to our girl, while his cock is buried in her mouth, does little to stop my need. The only way I know that he has pulled himself free from her throat is that our girl's moans and groans and cries are now not muted around his cock. Hearing her cries from the hits of the paddle does nothing to deter me, I land another ten before dropping the paddle next to my whip. Not stopping before my balls are slapping against her clit as I am buried to the hilt inside her tight pussy. Grabbing her hips up tighter, I drive into her deep steadying her with my grip.

Seeing Country climbing off of the bed, I know that I should stop before I am cumming, but I can't. I pound into her a handful of times more before I hear her pleading to come and as I give her permission, I am erupting into her growling out my release as her pussy convulses around my cock. Needing a minute, I lean down on our girl for a long moment before she wiggles beneath me, asking to be freed from the restraints binding her to the bed.

Standing up quickly, Country joins me in helping to free our girl and rubbing over the marks that are now on her wrists. As we lay her down onto the bed, the small bump in her belly, has my cock throbbing like it didn't just empty its load. Running my hands over the bump, I glance at Country and know with his smile, he is thinking the same thing that I am.

OURS!

CHAPTER
TWENTY

HEATHER

As I am situated onto the bed, I look up and see the love and want that is spilling from the two men in front of me. As Johnathan and Wayne run their hands over my body, paying special attention to the bump that has started to show itself, I feel nothing but cherished. As Johnathan pushes me onto my side, Wayne lays in front of me kissing and cuddling into me. Johnathan must grab up the salve, rubbing gently across my ass and thighs, it only stings for the first few moments, and then the numbing agent takes over and I feel only pleasure. As Wayne's hands explore my breasts, nipples, and finally my pussy, I moan and writhe under his touch. The more I moan the closer I am to the brink, and that is when the movements from Wayne are matched from behind by Johnathan. Johnathan pulls my top leg up and over his own, so that my legs are spread wide for him, and his hands.

As one of his hands starts moving over my top hip, he heads straight for my pussy. Stroking through my pussy, I find myself needy and only these two can answer my body's demands. Johnathan moves his knees, hiking my leg up further causing me to open up to them more. Driving two fingers into my pussy without much warning, quickly adding a third. Pumping into me a few times, he withdraws his fingers and I am at a loss, moaning and whining I feel a sharp slap to my ass before a deep laugh from behind.

"My Little Spitfire wants more, huh? Wayne our girl is ready for us and I am fucking ready to be buried inside of her."

Shifting me on the bed, I am in Johnathan's arms for only moments before I am laid on top of Wayne and impaled on his waiting cock. As I slowly, adjust and start to move, I feel hands roaming over my freshly whipped ass.

"My marks look good on you, Little Spitfire. No one other than me or Wayne will ever be buried inside of you or mark this beautiful flesh again." Running a slow hand over my spine, I begin to pick up my pace on Wayne's cock, before Johnathan's hands are on my stomach tracing the stretch marks that have started to form. I feel his breath on my ear before he chuckles then growls out, "Well, except our babies, that is."

Shaking my head at his idea of a joke, I almost forget that there is a cock buried inside of me, that is until I feel Wayne's hands on my hips, pushing me up and pulling me back onto him. After he has me screaming out my orgasm, I feel the bed sink behind me, knowing my men are claiming me together tonight. Wayne and Johnathan have taken me together plenty, and they are always very in tune with my pleasure and pain in the moment. Not waiting to give me anything that they see might be too much.

Drifting off to sleep, I think back to that first night they took me together. The night that everything changed between us, that night is something that will never leave my mind.

I don't notice the extra security until we are coming out of the room that Johnathan and Wayne had their way with me in for the last few hours. It has me wondering if something else has happened, since I got that note and the phone call. I think that they would have told me, if something had, but who knows if that is actually the case.

Walking towards the bar I see Peach with a sub that I have seen around a time or two, I think her name is Nichole. They are both sitting enjoying their drinks, old fashions if I know Peach, putting a hand to my belly, I know it will be at least six more months before I am in her seat again. Looking to my Masters, with a nod I am granted permission to head over to the girls and see what has happened since we have left the main room. Looking towards me, Peach is off her chair in a second throwing her arms around me, before rubbing a hand over my belly.

"Congrats, Heather. I am so happy for you, I heard about the baby and the guys asking you to marry them." Grabbing for my hand she pulls the hand towards her face looking at the ring the men have given to me. "OH Fuck, it's gorgeous, Heather. I can't believe that Bull and Country had this made for you. It matches your collar so nicely," running a finger over the collar as well, she smiles wide before going on. "You are so deserving of this, sweets. You and Sophie deserve to have nothing but happiness after all the shit you have, and are still going through from what I hear."

"Thanks so much, Becca, I don't know if I agree that I deserve these men, but I am not going to let them go." Smiling wide, I look towards her friend and pull my hand away from Becca before extending it to her friend. "I'm Heather, I don't think that we have ever officially met before."

Her friend wraps her hand around mine smiling wide as she speaks softly, "Hi, I'm Niki, I've seen you around a couple times before. It's nice to finally be introduced though, I like knowing the girls around places like this." Looking between myself and Peach she goes on, "I think that I might have even seen you around Club Coquin if I'm not mistaken."

Not remembering this woman from Club Coquin, I say the only thing I can think of, "Oh wow, you lived in New Orleans?" Thinking it odd, that I don't remember this girl, I think that I will call Mistress Diamond, and inquire about her. Not knowing what else to say, I stick with the old cliché, "I guess it really is a small world after all, huh?"

Wanting to ask more about our shared history, I am cut off as Johnathan and Wayne both surround me. "Spitfire, we need to go. Bull will take you up to the hospital, it seems that Ember and Doc's little Dalia has decided to come meet everyone a little early. At least she waited until after her mommy and daddy were finally married, I guess." He says with a chuckle before he goes on. "It also seems that your friend Sara has decided to go speak with her daddy, and Gun has called in for some backup, so I am headed up that way to help out." Looking towards Peach and Niki, Country turns back to me, pulling me into him before taking my mouth with his own. "Don't go anywhere without Bull, one of the other brothers, or a prospect, Heather. I am not letting Zack get anywhere near you and neither will Bull, or any of our brothers. I already had Prez send a couple guys over to Irene's to keep an eye on the kids, because Preach is heading up North with us."

"Ok, Wayne." Running a hand over the bump that is still only beginning to show itself, he places his hand on top of mine.

"We will all be okay. Don't worry about me. Go to the hospital and make sure that Doc, Ember, and Dalia are all doing good. It's going to be a long night for me, but I'll see you soon. I love you, Spitfire."

"I love you," is all I get out before I am stepping towards him kissing him on the lips.

As he pulls away from me, I am surrounded by Johnathan's arms and held tight. His voice is the only thing that puts me at ease, "Little Spitfire, he will be fine. They have to go get Sara out of a mess, that should have been dealt with long ago. Let's get over to the hospital."

"Ok," is all I can manage to say as he leads me towards the door, and into my truck. Strapping me in tightly, I know that until Zack is dealt with, we will find no peace.

CHAPTER TWENTY ONE

BULL

As the weeks pass most everything goes back to normal. Dalia was born about four weeks early, but is a fighter and had little problems after those first few days in the NICU. Adjusting to her new life, as a spoiled princess to the Devil's Iron, is something that one of our babies will need to take lessons in. The next day when Prez called Church we brought Heather becoming our ol' lady to the table and there was not a brother against it.

We found out about a month after Heather found out that she was pregnant that we were having twins. A boy and a girl. I am not sure how Country and I are going to handle raising twins but we have the best ol' lady around to help teach us how to do it right.

Heather has been under constant supervision since the first note from Zack came, and that is going on six weeks. If Country or I are not with her, another brother or a prospect is. We have been searching for Zack, but been coming up short. He has sent three more notes, untraceable, and made two more phone calls, both of which, thankfully, were only heard by me and Country. We know that if we just wait, he will slip up eventually. We are both just hoping it happens soon. Heather is due in four months, and we want to be sure to have this shit wrapped up tight before our babies come and join us.

As the beginning of April comes, we get a break and find Zack hiding out in a shithole on the outskirts of Chicago. The shit that we have found out during the long weeks since he first reached out to Heather in February is that he must of fucking hit rock bottom or fell the fuck off his rocker. In the past two years, he has gotten fired from his job, lost a girlfriend and kid, and lost most of his family's money trying to track down Heather and Sophie.

Not wanting to wait, as soon as Country and I get his location we call Prez and let him know the situation. He is quick to come, along with Doc and Tank to help us teach this fucking guy some fucking manners when it comes to our woman. We wait down the block until we see the three bikes coming down the street before we head to his house. Parking in front we make our way to the door, which we open for ourselves.

Finding Zack laid out on the couch, we waste no time letting him know the score.

"Fucking piece of shit. You think that you can threaten our ol' lady and our daughter?"

"Fuck!" Zack screams loudly getting up off the couch before trying to run for the door. Doc, lands a punch to his gut and tosses him back to the couch. "Fuck you! Fucking biker pieces of shit, my daughter shouldn't be anywhere near you fucking pieces of scum."

Landing a left hook to his jaw, Country begins to speak, "Shut the fuck up, before you talk yourself into a hole, you piece of shit. We are just here to let you know that you need to get your ass back down South and keep it there. You were nothing more than a fucking donor for Sophie. She is our daughter and you would do well to remember that." Landing another blow to Zack, I move up and tap Country out, wanting my turn at this piece of shit as well.

"Stay the fuck away from our woman and kids. This is the only warning you will get, if we find out that you have reached out to either of them again-" I accentuate every word with a blow to his gut. "YOU. WILL. FUCKING. DIE."

Each of my brothers takes a go with him, and we drop him off on a bus back to Texas a little worse for wear. I am sure that he has at least two broken ribs, maybe a broken wrist, and looks like he got hit by a fucking Mack truck.

We sent a prospect to follow the bus, and were told that he didn't get off the fucking bus until his final stop in Texas. The prospect said, he went to the hospital then to his parent's house, where he didn't come out much for the first two weeks that he was there. The prospect was on him a total of two months and never gave us any word that Zack wasn't doing exactly what we had asked of him.

Staying the fuck outta Chicago, and away from Heather and Sophie. The only flag that went up was right before we pulled the prospect back up to Chicago in the beginning of May. When Zack started going to a bar that was well known as a biker bar. Not knowing what he could possibly be thinking or wanting, we decide to leave well enough alone and just put the word out to all our chapters, to keep an eye out for him.

Both mine and Country's minds are put at ease knowing that Zack is outta the picture and we start settling into our family even more. Once we got settled into the house after the remodeling was done, we have really managed to come up with a good hierarchy. Country and I take turns doing runs when needed for the Devil's Iron so that Sophie and Heather are never alone. We all share in most of the household shit, especially with Heather getting as far along with the twins as she is. Our lives are perfect and we know that as soon as our twins come into our lives and we are finally able to marry Heather nothing will come between us.

Needing one final night out before the babies come, we leave Sophie with Grams for the night, around the middle of June, deciding to have our way with our woman. She is due in another month or so, but the doctor has put our minds at ease about our sessions we share with her. This might be the last one we have before the babies come and we want to make sure it is something that will last on all of our minds during the weeks that we will not be able to take our woman the way we want.

Heading into The Dungeon on a Tuesday night is something that we would almost never do, but seeing that our woman is feeling good and we had a sitter, we decide to go for it. As we make our way through the door, we are greeted by Shadow. "Bull, Country, Heather. It's nice to see you. It has been quite a while." Stepping towards our woman, he places a gentle hand on her belly before reaching his arms around her in a hug. The growl that comes outta my mouth is matched by one from Country, and Shadow pulls back slightly. "Fuck guys, I haven't seen her in weeks and you are so fucking jealous, just like that first time. Don't worry, Peach would have my balls if I ever thought of it. Speaking of Peach," turning towards our girl, "You haven't heard from her today have you Heather? I let her session with Niki outside of The Dungeon last night and haven't heard from her today."

Shaking her head Heather answers quickly, "No, I haven't. That's weird, she knows that she should check in. Let me know when you hear from her please."

"No problem, I'm sure I am just being over protective. Go have fun tonight."

Heading straight to a room, we waste no time getting our girl naked. Tying her arms to the bed, is the only position that she can be in this far along, and we use it to our advantage. While I prop a pillow under her head, Country wastes no time attacking her sweet cunt with his mouth and hands. Seeing our girl screaming out an orgasm within short moments, I find myself needing to be buried deep down her throat. Getting onto the bed I crawl over to her and lay so that my cock is resting on the pillow where her head has just moved away from. She locks eyes with me, licking her lips before taking me deep down her throat. She wastes no time, and starts doing exactly what I have taught her that I like, taking me in all the way until she gags on my cock. Within two minutes I feel her humming out her orgasm as I cum along with her. Pulling my cock out of her mouth, I pause as she licks it clean before swapping places with Country.

As Country assumes the position on the bed that I was just in, I grab up our Little Spitfire's paddle, and start in on her lush globes. After a few minutes warming her up I decide that our girl should have a little treat tonight and move over to the closet. Taking out the new cat o' nines that I have purchased, I let it thud against my palm a few times before moving back to the bed.

"Spitfire, you have been a good girl for us these past few months and we have been so wrapped up in getting ready for the twins, I think we have been ignoring you. Have you earned this new cat o' nines that I have bought for you? I think that you deserve the pleasure that you will find in it, don't you Wayne?"

"God," is grunted out as Heather swallows Country down as I land the first hit. "Give it to her, Johnathan. Because the way she takes my cock when you are fucking working her over is unmatched. Do your worst to our girl and she will only be that much more giving." Seeing his hands thread into her hair guiding her mouth down his cock, only drives me on.

Landing a total of ten strokes to her ass and thighs, I see her cream slipping down her legs on the last stroke and know that we need to get her arms down. She is starting to wiggle her fingers to get the feeling back to them and that is one of her tells that it is time to move her body. Dropping the cat o'nine I move to her wrists quickly removing the binding from them before rubbing the soreness out.

Laying her out on the bed facing Country, he takes her mouth with his own. I grab for the salve before applying a liberal amount to her ass and thighs. As I finish up, Heather is impaling herself on Country's cock and I feel no need to wait. I bury myself deep inside her ass and Country and I use our woman well. Not stopping until we are all shattering together.

Pulling out of her, is the worst feeling, but grabbing her up in between us is one of the best and we lay there wrapped around our girl for almost an hour, before we make our way to the sink to get cleaned up. Finishing first I am the one tasked with cleaning our girl up tonight, and I take my time washing her and soothing the aches away. When we use her in this way as we did tonight, she is left with no thoughts that we do not treasure her in every way afterwards.

CHAPTER
TWENTY TWO

HEATHER

Looking around as we enter the main room, the atmosphere is definitely different than it would be on almost any other night of the week. There are not so many Tuesday evening kinksters it seems. We must have been in our room for the session for two hours or so, and it is still early in the night, but fuck is it dead at the bar. Stretching my sore muscles as we move further into the room, I see Peach at the bar and ask my Masters if I may go speak with her and they allow it, needing to find their brothers before we make our way home.

"Peach, hey lady. Where's Niki, she has seemed to be your constant companion these last few months," I say touching her shoulder as I plop myself in the chair next to her. As she slowly turns to me, I notice the tear stains on her cheeks and move quickly to wipe them away. Looking around, I see a few couples in various situations around the room, and then I see the only person that I think could have caused this pain. I see Shadow moving slowly down the hallway away from the bar, with his head dropped down. "Sweets, what's going on? Did something happen with Shadow, I thought you two were finally coming into your own. That you had finally worked through the shit between you two and were happy."

Moving to speak, her words are cut off with more tears and small gasps. Reaching my arm around her, I pull her into me as she cries. The only words that I am able to make out, are "baby and daddy." What that means, I am not sure, I don't know what the fuck has happened, but I know that if this girl needs my help to get away from here, there will be no one and nothing that stops me. As Johnathan and Wayne walk towards us, I take a protective stance in front of Peach and they notice my movements in a second.

Looking down the hall, they see Shadow retreating and look towards me with wide eyes, "Spitfire, you should not get involved in this. It has nothing to do with you." Country reaches out to me as he tries to speak again.

Meeting his eyes, I pull away from his reach and cock my head to the side saying, "I am and it does."

Shaking his head, Country looks to Bull and I see an unspoken exchange take place. Nodding towards Country, Bull reaches out to both Peach and I as I am scooped up under his arm, "Either way, we need to head home."

Taking a deep breath, Peach speaks slowly, "I will be fine to get home, go get home with your men." Placing a hand on my humongous stomach, "You and those babies of yours need all the rest you can get."

Tightening my hold on her, I let her know that is not an option. "You are not going home alone. You will stay with us tonight. I'm not sure what is going on with you, but I know, sure as fuck, that I am not leaving you alone." Moving a few steps, I turn back to my men, "We are going to change and then we will meet you outside of the locker room in fifteen? She is coming home with us tonight, and that is not open for discussion."

The men answer in tandem, and then head off to get changed as we move to our locker room. Striding towards my locker, I have my club wear off and am pulling the sweater over my head and pulling up my yoga pants within three minutes flat. Nothing is going to feel as good as sinking into that huge bed with my men when we get home. It really does pay to have a spare set of clothes here at The Dungeon for myself. Turning around I see Peach struggling to get the outfit she is wearing off, and that is when I notice something on her flesh.

"Peach" comes out softly as I reach out and lightly run a hand over the bruise that I would recognize anywhere. A bruise made out of hate and anger. A bruise made not from a paddle, a crop, or a whip, but instead from a fist. Taking the two steps to close the distance between us, I help her out of her skirt and top, I see that her torso is covered and it looks as if someone has used her as a punching bag. Moving to grab up her pants, I drop down to my knees so she doesn't need to move any more than necessary to get into them. Moving back towards her sweatshirt, I do the same by hopping up onto the bench so that she doesn't need to bend over to get it on.

Not being able to stop myself, I look her in the eyes and ask, "Did Shadow do this to you, sweets?"

Shaking her head adamantly, I soften knowing he is not the one who has done this on her. "Who, then?"

As she looks up into my eyes, she holds them for only a few moments before dropping them away and saying a name, I would have never guessed.

"Zack."

That is all I remember, before blacking out.

CHAPTER TWENTY THREE

COUNTRY

Waiting outside of the women's locker room, I glance down and see that it is going on fifteen minutes that they have been in there. Not wanting to wait any longer I push the door open, and yell, "Peach, Heather, you in here." Hearing crying, I slam the door open without thought, and turn to see Peach lying over Heather on the floor.

"Help Country, she just passed out, I don't know what the fuck happened, she was talking to me one minute and then the next she fucking fell down. Help her."

With that, I glance behind me and see Bull running towards us. "Call for an ambulance and get them here fucking quick." Is all I can manage before a cry rips through me and I scoop our girl up in my arms, carrying her out of the locker room. Seeing a couch nearby I place her gently down on that before I am able to look our girl over and see if there is something truly wrong. Seeing Shadow coming back down the hallway, I notice an exchange between him and Peach before I see Heather's eyes start to open, the smile on my face at her consciousness, is ripped away as she says only one word.

"Zack"

Not knowing what she means or what the fuck is going on, I take her hands in mine, and start in on her. "What are you talking about Heather? We scared the fuck outta him those months back, and he left with his tail between his legs. Did he speak with you again? If he fucking did I will go to fucking Texas and teach him a lesson that he will not soon forget. There is no way that anyone would have allowed him anywhere near this fucking club, all the security has his picture and know that he could be a fucking problem and have known that since the first note all those months ago." Reaching his hand up to me he strokes down my face slowly saying, "No one would've let him anywhere near any of our girls, we protect what is ours."

With that a cry comes out from Peach who is still crouched down by Heather's head. She speaks with such venom, I am not sure I would have thought possible of her during the years that I have known her. "No, but they would've let the sick son of a bitch near someone that didn't mean so much, Right?" Is all she is able to get out before taking off down the hallway and heading out into the cold Chicago air. That is when I hear a roar coming from Shadow, and see him slam a vase against the wall, followed by his fists.

Bull speaks loudly, "Knock it the fuck off, old man. What the fuck is going on?" Looking from me to Shadow and then to our woman he goes on, "Could someone please explain this shit to me!"

Shadow moves back towards us before speaking. "Peach was attacked last night. It was my fault, that I didn't know enough to vet that fucking bitch out better. I didn't even think twice about letting her out with Niki to test my Peach's pain. That was not what fucking Zack had in mind for her though. She ended up being used by some fucking guys she swore wore Demon Riders cuts."

My eyes go wide hearing the name of the Demon Riders, the club that my father was part of, that I had grown up with. What the fuck would they be doing up here? They have no fucking chapters anywhere up North, and I know for a fact that they don't travel over the Mason/Dixon before summer is in full swing.

That is unless they have come up here to get vengeance for a fallen brother. I should have guessed that a seventeen-year-old trying to cover up a murder, especially the murder of his father, the fucking President of their MC would not get over on them. Although after the first few months, hell the first few years, with no word or contact I really had thought I might have gotten away with it.

Now I have brought down this fucking war on my brothers, on Peach, and it looks like maybe even my woman.

FUCK!

Shadow takes off after Peach quickly when she runs, as I wonder what happened to her last night. Making sure that Bull stays with our girl, I move over to the bar pulling my cell phone out as I go. Dialing Prez, I know that the shit I am going to tell him, will not settle well with him. Gruffly he answers, "What's going on brother?"

"Well, Prez, I think I got just that. We need to talk."

"Yeah? I heard something was going down at The Dungeon tonight, is that what this is about?"

"Kinda."

"Okay, well I'll meet you at the clubhouse in twenty, okay?"

"Yes, Prez. See you there." Closing the phone, I shove it into my pocket, before walking back over to the group surrounding Heather. Standing by Bull I quietly let him know that I am talking with Prez tonight and need him to watch over our girl until I can get home. Bending down, I am whispering in Heather's ear as I speak so no one else can hear.

"Spitfire, I will never let him or anyone hurt you, neither will Bull or any of our brothers. I know that you are confused, and so are we, thinking that Zack had anything to do with this attack on Peach. We will find out what happened and we will make it right." Stroking a hand over her hair, I notice the look of indifference in her as I add, "He will know that you are off limits and that he should have never come back at you or any of us. I have to go speak with Prez, Bull will be here to take you home whenever you're ready. Just know that we will not let you outta our sights until this shit has come to a solution." Leaning down I kiss her hair and then her cheek before taking her mouth with mine. The passion is lacking but I know it is due to the night that has played itself out before us.

"I love you, Spitfire," are the last words I say to our girl before I turn around and head for the exit. Moving towards the door, I catch Shadow sitting on the floor in-between Peach's feet, with his arms wrapped around her. "We will need to speak with her, when she is calmed down brother. I am heading to the clubhouse now, maybe you could bring her over?"

"Will do, Country." As I start to walk away, he stops me. "Country, there is something else you should know."

Looking over my shoulder I ask, "What's that, Shadow?"

"Seems that sub Nicole was working with Zack and the Demon Riders. She is the one that lured Peach away last night."

"Understood, Shadow." Is all I can say as I shift back around and head through the door. Getting on my bike, I don't notice the van that pulls out behind me. I am too wrapped up in the thoughts of Zack and the Demon Riders to notice when it pulls up alongside of me. I am too distracted to notice the door opening or the gun that is pointed at me as I ride.

You know what I'm not too distracted to pay attention to though?

When the first bullet rips through me.

COMING SOON....
DEVIL'S IRON MC BOOK 7
HEATHERED COUNTRY PART 2

~CHAPTER 1
BULL

I know that Zack must have come straight into The Dungeon to get Peach or had someone working with him, and that isn't sitting well with me. I try to think about what new people have been at The Dungeon, especially the ones hanging around my woman. My mind drifts to the only new people that have been showing their faces consistently around Heather the last few months.

Fucking Niki

If he has been following after Heather for these last few months, why did he pick now to come at us? Maybe because she is so far gone with the babies? As I look towards my woman, who is still laying on the couch it takes me only an instant to notice the blood seeping onto the crotch of her gray yoga pants. When realization hits me, it's about the time that a scream rips through her like I have never heard before. As my eyes meet hers, she tells me something that makes no sense.

"THEIR COMING!"

I look up into her eyes and see pain that has never been there before, as she squeezes tightly to my hand and starts panting. Just as the realization that our woman is in labor hits me, the doors to The Dungeon swing wide, and five men enter.

Four men wearing Demon Riders cuts and the man I thought we had dealt with months ago.

Zack

… TO BE CONTINUED….

42359638R00121

Made in the USA
Middletown, DE
10 April 2017